Black and White and Red all Over

A Summer McCloud paranormal mystery

Nikki Broadwell

Airmid Publishing
Tucson, Arizona

Black and White and *Red* all Over

Copyright © 2016. Nikki Broadwell

This is a work of fiction. All names, characters places and ideas presented here are products of the author's imagination.

Formatting by Wild Seas Formatting

ISBN-: 978-0-9906697-8-4

Acknowledgements:

A heartfelt thank you to Rob Hall, for all his generous help regarding forensic evidence. Without his expertise my homicide detective would have been wandering around in the dark without a clue.

1

"You have to help me find a dress!" Agnes cried. "The wedding is less than six weeks away!"

I smiled at my best friend who had turned into a nervous Nellie about her upcoming wedding. "You told me you didn't want a traditional dress so I think the second hand store on the other end of town is our best bet. They have good quality vintage clothes." The small town of Ames, Connecticut was too small to have a lot to choose from. Agnes had a unique style all her own with beautiful and artistic tattoos of goddesses up and down her arms and straight twenties hairstyle. Any dress she picked would have to be unusual. "You do know you can't have a black dress?" I teased. Black was Agnes's favorite color as evidenced by what she was wearing— long black tunic over black tights and high black boots.

She stuck her tongue out at me. "I don't want a black dress, Summer, but I also don't want white."

Her petite frame would look good in just about anything, I thought, staring at her straight dark hair and almond shaped brown eyes. I was several inches taller, with less grace about me. I often felt gawky and clumsy next to her.

"And I also don't want some ripped piece of you-know-what," she continued. "I want something elegant and classy."

"I know that," I snapped, becoming a tiny bit annoyed. "You asked for my help and this is what I suggest. I've bought several really nice dresses from Once Again. And if we don't find anything there we can look in a catalogue."

Agnes flopped onto the loveseat, her gaze going round my living room. "Are you sure you want to host the rehearsal dinner? This place is kind of small."

I had to admit the cottage I'd inherited from my mother was not very large, but if I moved the furniture around there was plenty of room for a dining table to accommodate the few members of the wedding party. "You said I was the only bridesmaid, or should I say maid of honor? And with David, Sam's brother, their parents and Tom, that's four more—who's standing up for Sam?"

Agnes stared at the ceiling, her hands clasping and unclasping nervously. "I thought I told you already. Jerry's his best man."

I should have guessed. My former boyfriend Jerry and I had not spoken in over nine months. I'd seen him around town once or twice, but we'd studiously avoided each other. "I forgot." I noticed her worried look. "I'm over him, Agnes. It's fine. I'm with Tom now."

"Tom's nice," Agnes said, unenthusiastically. "But I miss you and Jerry." She looked over at me noticing my distressed expression. "I'm sorry, Summer—didn't mean to open old wounds."

I made a feeble attempt to smile, trying not to burst into tears. In all honesty I was not over Jerry and might never be. Tom was a nice enough man, and we had a lot of fun together, but Jerry was my soul mate.

Jerry Brady was a detective on the Ames police force, and Sam Anderson's partner, and because of my amateur sleuthing Jerry and I had worked on several cases together. Our rapport had been great until our last case, which ended with a psychopath in my house ready to kill me. If Jerry hadn't shown up at that precise moment I wouldn't be sitting here thinking about him. Jerry left my house that night with a murderer in tow, and I hadn't heard from him since. After all this time I still couldn't believe he'd never reached out. The idea of him here in my house, perhaps with a girlfriend on his arm, gave me a prickly feeling all over.

"Moving on with someone new is the best thing to do," Agnes continued, trying to make up for her earlier statement. "I'm sorry you'll have to be around Jerry for the rehearsal dinner and the wedding. But at least you'll have Tom for support."

I shook my head as though it meant nothing to me and went into the kitchen. "Wine?" I asked, holding up a bottle of white I'd recently purchased.

"If you insist," she grinned, joining me in the kitchen. "Sam's coming by in a while. Is that okay? He wants to go over the guest list again and he has some suggestions about the food."

"Sure." Somehow I'd been roped into being the wedding planner, a role that didn't fit me very well. I'd already contacted the newest and best restaurant in Ames, Saffron and Seaweed, about doing the food, but we hadn't finalized any of it yet. I opened the wine and poured it into two glasses, my mind on my store. Tarot and Tea was taking a back seat to my new duties and my customers were not happy when I closed early or opened late. I had to take time for my own business or I wouldn't be able to pay my bills.

This wedding had been the main focus of both our lives for months now and I was ready for it to be over.

The ballroom in the old age home had finally been remodeled and that's where the ceremony and the reception would take place. The turn-of-the-century Victorian building had been a project of Agnes's since the fall and now it was nearly completed. I was pleased that all the ghosts wandering around town could finally settle into their new/old digs. Douglas, a ghost and also Agnes's father, had remarked to me earlier today how glad he was. "The place is just the way it was nearly one hundred years ago," he'd told me when he came into Tarot and Tea. He would know, I'd thought to myself, trying to suppress a giggle.

In truth, I had no idea how old the man was, only that I liked him very much and that he had an elegant and old-fashioned way about him. He and Agnes's mother, a woman who'd been murdered here in Ames two years ago, had reconnected just before her death. Agnes still spoke about Serena Weatherby in hushed tones, gasping over the enormous inheritance Serena had left her. I figured she and Sam would buy some mansion to live in once they were married. I only hoped they would stay in Ames and not move to some swank section of New York too far away for me to visit. But then again I had a hard time imagining Sam quitting the police force. Being a detective was his life.

Douglas and Serena, Agnes's parents, had loved each other and apparently conceived a child after Douglas left the land of the living. Even with my own burgeoning psychic abilities I found this revelation disturbing. I wondered why Serena had never appeared to any of us after her demise. I had yet to ask Douglas if he ever saw her.

A hundred guests were coming to the wedding, Sam's friends and family who made up a cast of thousands, as well as Agnes's college friends she'd lost touch with who were now married with children. She told me she was hoping to reconnect now that she was about to join them in the respectable institution of matrimony.

Agnes had always been a free spirit and that's why we'd become such good friends. This new side of her, that seemed to think that getting married placed her in an entirely different social stratum, bothered me greatly. She was my best friend and I relied on her to continue in that regard. We still went to our monthly coven meetings on the full moon, and I hoped we would continue to do so after her marriage.

We had consumed half the bottle by the time Sam arrived, his expression grim.

"What's wrong?" Agnes asked, jumping up from the couch.

He rubbed a hand across his clean-shaven face. "There's been an incident," he began, slanting a glance toward me. "There was a shooting a couple of hours ago at Riverview Elementary."

My mouth dropped open in horror. These school shootings had been happening all over the country but I never thought they would occur in our sleepy village of Ames, Connecticut. I clutched my glass and tried not to see the ravaged faces of the poor children.

"Five kids and three teachers were shot today," he continued, slumping onto the couch. "It was a bloodbath."

Agnes's pale face turned whiter than usual, tears welling in her eyes. She sat next to Sam and turned toward me. "Summer, have you seen…?"

I knew what she was referring to and shook my head. Ghosts often talked to me but I had had no visits, at least not yet. "What happened?" I asked Sam, girding myself for what he would say.

"Some maniac came into the school with an assault rifle and just shot up the building. We have no motive, no name, and no understanding of where the shooter came from and or why he or she did what they did."

"Which teachers?" Agnes asked in a small voice. We both knew several teachers at the elementary school.

"Linda Moser and Gabby Cozens were killed— Maggie Johnson was shot but survived."

Agnes let out a wail. "I know them!"

"I do too," I said, moving next to her. She turned to face me and then we hugged, both of us in tears.

"None of the witnesses can remember what the shooter looked like or even if it was a he or a she. I find that odd, especially since two other teachers and Maggie witnessed the entire thing, not to mention the other twenty children who were in the classroom. The only thing they said was they thought the person had brown hair."

"Well, that narrows it down," I said.

Sam shot me a look. "It's a start and we have a sketch artist working with the witnesses."

"Linda and Gabby were coming to the wedding," Agnes said, pulling away to look at Sam again. "Did they die quickly? Don't tell me," she said a second later, holding up her hand. "Do you think we should postpone the wedding?"

"The wedding is over a month away, Agnes. I'm sure this will be wrapped up by then. And even if it isn't I don't think we should." Sam took hold of her hand, twining his fingers through hers. "I've got to get back to the police station. Jerry and I are leading the investigation."

So he and Jerry were partners again. Last I'd heard

Jerry wasn't even back to full duty. But then again it had been months since his mental collapse after the last case we'd worked on together. I wondered if the chief had insisted he see a therapist.

"And Summer, you may be called in."

"Called in—why?"

"Your psychic skills. The chief mentioned you during our planning meeting."

I shook my head. "Unless one of the ghosts contacts me I can do nothing. It isn't like I go into a trance and know what happened."

"Sorry to hear that," he said, regarding me with a somber expression. He kissed Agnes before he stood and headed for the door. "But please let me know if you dream anything or one of them visits you. We could really use some help on this one." He opened the door and closed it behind him. I heard the squad car start up and then the squeal of one of the belts as he put it in gear and headed away.

I felt ill as I pictured Linda and Gabby lying on the classroom floor in a pool of blood. They were both my age, late twenties. It suddenly occurred to me that I was turning thirty this year, a milestone I wasn't looking forward to. But then I thought of them again, their lives cut short, and I mentally reprimanded myself. And Gabby had a little girl, Mary. Was her child one of the five victims? And what about Maggie—did her boy survive? I raced to the door and flung it open, but Sam was long gone.

2

Agnes stared at me from the loveseat, her eyes glazed with unshed tears. "How can I concentrate on my wedding now?" she whispered. "I can't imagine what they went through." And then she was sobbing with her head in her hands. "I have to postpone—who wants to celebrate when seven people are lying dead in the morgue?"

Even though I grieved for Gabby and Linda and the families who had lost their children, I was dry-eyed. Maybe it was the knowledge that there really was life after death—a fact that had become only too clear during the past year. Maybe Douglas could talk with Agnes. If anyone could make her feel better it was him`. "The shooter will be in jail by the time your wedding day comes and those kids will have moved on."

Agnes looked up, her face wet with tears. "How can you be so matter-of-fact about this? These are our kids— the ones who belong to people we know. Their lives are shattered forever and ever! And what about Gabby and Sally? They have family here."

I stared at her but couldn't think what to say to make her feel better. There were some happenings in life that only time could erase—and this was one of them.

Once Agnes left for home I cleaned up and let Cutty, my scruffy wire-haired terrier mix, in from the back yard.

I fed him his dinner and then poured myself another glass of wine, trying to get the images I'd conjured out of my mind. When my cell phone rang I nearly jumped out of my skin. But when I looked at the caller I.D. I was even more surprised—it was Jerry.

"Is Sam still there?" he asked as soon as I answered.

"No, he left forty-five minutes ago. Did you try his cell?"

I heard him sigh before he said, "Of course I tried his cell. I guess you heard about the shooting."

"Sam told us. Do you have any leads?"

"Not yet, but I'm hoping we can get the witnesses to remember something."

"Maybe someone should hypnotize them."

Jerry scoffed. "You always go for the weird stuff first, don't you?"

"You didn't think it was weird when I talked to the dead woman on our last case."

"Didn't I?" he asked sarcastically.

"Jerry, I don't want to have this conversation. If you feel like talking about what happened between us, call me. Otherwise leave me alone." I pressed the end button and threw my phone across the room. Luckily it landed on the rug and didn't crack.

I looked up when Tom opened the front door, his eyes widening when he saw the expression on my face. "What happened?"

After I explained about the shooting he took me in his arms. "I'm sorry, Summer. If I can do anything please let me know."

I held onto him for a few minutes, trying to calm my erratic heartbeat caused by Jerry's phone call. When we finally pulled apart he took hold of my elbows, searching my face. "What else happened?"

"Isn't a school shooting enough?"

"I know you and there's something you aren't telling me."

I let out a long sigh. "If you must know Jerry just called. He was looking for Sam."

"And?"

"And nothing. I told him to leave me alone."

Tom seemed to relax. He headed into the kitchen and held the wine bottle up. "How much have you had?"

Tom monitored me like a mother hen, something I did not appreciate. "I shared it with Agnes and Sam," I told him before moving toward the refrigerator. "Do you want me to fix dinner?"

"I'm sorry. It's just that you went through that heavy drinking period when we first got together. My father's a recovering alcoholic and it worries me when someone I care about abuses alcohol."

"I know all about your father, Tom. And my drinking was due to what happened between Jerry and me—you know that. We certainly discussed it ad nauseum. And I would hardly call my drinking 'abusing alcohol'."

Tom softened his expression. "Pour me a glass, would you?"

"You didn't answer my question about food. Is that why you dropped by?"

Tom took the glass I held out. "I wish you'd let me move in. We've been together for months now. It seems silly for me to rent that house when we spend nearly every night together."

I stared out the window at the catkins that had appeared on the maples in the last week. It was the beginning of May but I didn't feel my usual enthusiasm about the nicer weather or the idea of picnics, swimming in the quarry or any of the other things the warmer months had always meant to me. This time of year brought back the memory of Jerry's and my last case, the trip we'd made to the beach community of Watch Hill that turned into a murder investigation. And at the end of it all Jerry had decided he hated the sight of me.

I was also upset about the shooting and confused about what was going on between Tom and me. I liked him well enough, but I had no desire to have him move in. To my mind our relationship was casual and would probably never move past where it was now. He'd been hounding me about moving in for weeks and I'd been putting off talking to him about what was going on between us. I turned to face him. "As you know Jerry lived here. I'm not ready to take that kind of step again, at least not now." I glanced at the end of the counter where Jerry's espresso machine had lived, remembering the taste of the coffee we shared each morning. Now I made the ubiquitous coffee machine coffee and drank it only because it woke me up in the morning.

"You aren't over him, are you? That's why you seem so standoffish and cold. I thought I could make you happy."

I glanced at him noticing the hurt expression on his face. "You have made me happy."

Tom shook his head and put his empty wine glass down on the butcher block. "Call me when you've figured it out," he said, frowning at me. And then he headed toward the door.

I watched him go, knowing that all I had to do was say his name, but something kept me silent. The front door slammed and I heard his car start up. The calm I felt after his car drove away answered an unasked question. I wanted to process the shooting and Jerry's call, in that order. And I also needed to ponder why I had never told

Tom that I could see and talk to ghosts, as well as use the ether as my own private method of transport. Of course the astral traveling had only happened once, but I felt certain that if I were about to be smothered in an airless room again, the ability would be there. I pushed the horrible image from my mind, returning my attention to Tom. In all the months we'd been together I'd never really let him in.

I was deeply asleep when I heard Cutty barking. For a few moments I incorporated the sound into my dream as I ran down a silvery beach after my dog. But then the barking turned frantic and my eyes flew open. Was there someone in the house? I realized with a start that I'd forgotten to lock the door after Tom left. I slid out of bed, pulled my gun out of the bedside table, and moved as quietly as I could toward the living room. From the kitchen I could see Cutty standing by the lumpy dark shapes of my loveseat and chair, his barking continuing unabated. As my eyes adjusted I let out a gasp. A woman stood in the middle of my living room, her translucent image moving in and out of focus. "Who's there?" I asked, trying to keep my voice from shaking.

She seemed in her late thirties, long brown hair in waves around her shoulders. Her eyes were dark holes, her mouth moving as she tried to speak. She was wearing a wrap-around housedress in a checked fabric that belonged in the forties. Behind her was a window that didn't exist in my reality and through the panes I saw old airplanes in formation, the engines throbbing dully in my ears. "Who are you and what do you want?" I asked, holding the gun out in front of me.

When she put her hand to her mouth I could see

straight through it. Her eyes were now frightened pools. I placed the gun on the butcher block and moved closer. "What do you want?"

By now Cutty had stopped barking but he was still staring at the apparition with more than his normal intensity. She looked from him to me and then opened her mouth again, but I couldn't hear what she was saying. I moved closer, trying to read her lips, but it was impossible. She stared at me with a sad expression and then slowly dissipated until there was nothing left except the window and the disturbing low hum coming from the planes. And then even that was gone. I sat on the couch and hoped she'd come back, but an hour went by with no sign of her.

I woke in the morning with a stiff neck from sleeping at an odd angle on the couch. Cutty was curled up next to me, his bright eyes popping open as soon as I stirred. I had to find out who she was.

3

"You've finally deigned to open your store."

I turned to the gray-haired woman who looked to be in her late seventies. Mrs. Browning was an enigma. I assumed she was a ghost but had no real proof of such. She was a member of the coven and seemed to know about things before they happened, and also seemed a contemporary of Douglas who I knew for sure was a ghost. "Sorry I didn't open yesterday, Mrs. Browning," I said, turning the key in the lock. "But if you want to blame someone, blame Agnes. She's the one taking up all my time."

Mrs. Browning harrumphed and walked past me into the store, disappearing into the shelves where I kept the goddess books. I closed the door behind me and turned on the light before greeting my store cat, Tabby. She rubbed against my legs, her purr of contentment making me smile. "How is your food supply?" I crooned, heading into the back to check her food and water dish.

When I came into the main store again several more people were wandering around. They were mostly regulars but I noticed a brown-haired woman who appeared to be in her sixties whom I didn't recognize. When she came up to the counter with a book in her hand I suppressed a gasp. She looked startlingly like the ghost from the night before.

She held the book out that had to do with life after death. "Did you hear about the horrible shooting yesterday?" she asked me.

I nodded. "It's probably the most horrific thing that's ever happened in Ames."

"Did you know the school building used to be a recruitment office? The army commandeered it before the Second World War."

"I didn't know that. Do you think it's significant?"

She shrugged, her brown eyes sliding away. "Just an interesting fact," she said, handing me her money.

After she left I had a sort of déjà vu experience, wondering if she could be related to my latest ghost. Unfortunately she hadn't given me a card so I didn't have her name.

When Mrs. Browning arrived with yet another goddess book to buy I asked if she recognized my earlier customer.

"Come to think of it, dear, she looked a lot like Sadie Cumberland. But Sadie died eons ago."

"Do you know anything about this Sadie?"

The older woman frowned. "Poor Sadie lost both her son and her husband to the war. It was very tragic."

"The Second World War?"

Mrs. Browning looked up at me, her eyes rheumy. "Why of course, dear. Did you think I was talking about WW1?"

I shrugged and rang her up, thinking about all the wars we'd been in since then, ticking them off in my mind.

The store was quiet when Douglas arrived. And, as usual, I had not seen him come through the door. "Just the person I want to see," I said, just before he moved into the shelves.

He turned his gray eyes on me. "Why is that?"

"You need to talk to your daughter. She's hysterical

about the shooting and I thought you might be able to calm her down."

Douglas frowned, his gaze going into the distance. "Terrible tragedy," he mumbled, "those young lives cut off before they could begin."

"But they're ghosts like you now, aren't they?"

Douglas met my gaze. "Not necessarily, Summer. When a life that young is taken, they often reincarnate. And when they do that they are gone from this realm until reborn."

"Oh. I thought…"

Douglas put his hand on my arm. "I will have a word with Agnes. I hope this terrible incident won't stop her from her wedding vows. I've looked so forward to it."

"Sam is determined to go through with it. He said he was sure this tragedy would be cleared up by then—at least the perpetrator brought to justice."

"I hope he's right. This is an odd one," Douglas said before walking away to peruse the essential oils.

I wanted to ask him what he meant but it was obvious he didn't want to discuss it any further. "Why hasn't Serena returned as a ghost?" I asked later when he brought up a small bottle of lavender. Serena was Agnes's mother, a woman who'd been murdered practically on the doorstep of my store and because of that I'd been at the top of the suspect list. She was also the love of Douglas's life.

Douglas looked startled for a moment. "I can't really tell you why. She may appear at some time in the future but so far I haven't seen her. I did hope…" he looked away, his gaze wistful.

"It would be nice if she could attend the wedding too. Agnes never got to know her own mother."

"Unfortunately I have no control over what happens

after death, my dear. Serena may still be in the bardo, for all I know."

"The bardo, what's that?"

"The bardo is the in-between place where spirits go after death. Serena may reincarnate instead of doing what I have done. Perhaps she will come back as Agnes's first child." He smiled and winked and took the wrapped package I handed him. When I looked up from the cash register a moment later he'd vanished.

I wondered if the dead person had any choice in the matter, or if it was just some willy-nilly sorting process that I didn't understand. And then I thought of the children and what he'd said about them—the parents who must be utterly devastated. I couldn't imagine who in Ames could have committed such a horrific act of violence. And it scared me to think we had that kind of a psychopath living among us.

Agnes called when I was walking home—nothing new since I heard from her nearly every day since I'd been roped into being her personal wedding consultant.

"Did you say something to Douglas?" she asked me breathlessly. "Because he came by the house and seemed determined to talk with me about what happened at the school. According to him the children will all reincarnate, and he said something about my mother too. He kind of freaked me out, Summer."

"Sorry, Agnes. I did mention that you were worried about going ahead with the wedding. He wanted to reassure you that these children are not gone."

"Of course they're gone! They aren't here in Ames anymore—how can he be so callous?"

"You have to remember where he's coming from—your father is a ghost. How can he look at things like you

21

and I do?"

There was silence as Agnes thought about this. "Okay, I'll give him that, but I'm sure the parents of the dead kids don't feel that way."

"I'm sure you're right unless they're extremely enlightened or Tibetan Buddhists or something. Douglas wants to encourage you and Sam to go ahead, okay?"

"Easy for you to say. My husband-to-be is the one working the damn case. I'll hear every horrid detail from now until they've solved it. And what's worse is all the fallout around town. Have you read the news?"

"No. I don't get the paper."

"Well, pick one up on your way home." When the call ended abruptly I looked around, realizing I had nearly reached my cottage. My feet seemed to have traversed the familiar sidewalks by themselves as I talked on the phone. When I entered my tiny yard a paper was lying on the walkway. The paperboy must have made a mistake, I thought, picking it up. I unfolded it, my gaze going to the large bold letters at the top of the page.

AMES CHILDREN SLAUGHTERED! Under the headline was a grainy picture that depicted the mayhem at the school. Thank goodness it was out of focus and in black and white, but I could still imagine the blood spread around the bodies that lay in various contorted configurations. I felt sick for a moment as I thought about the poor children who had witnessed their playmates being killed. The article went on:

A maniac, who still remains at large, has taken five of our children as well as two of our teachers from us. The police seem to be at a loss about the motivations or perpetrator of this heinous crime. Parents are petrified to let their children out of their sight until the killer is apprehended. Riverside

22

Elementary is closed until further notice.

I took the paper with me inside and threw it into the nearest wastebasket. These reporters weren't helping. Things were bad enough without adding fuel to the fire. I knew very well that most men here owned guns for hunting and many were gun collectors with assault rifles and other deadly weapons in their possession. What would happen if vigilantes began to comb the countryside searching for the person who did this? When my cell phone rang I was sure it was Agnes again, but instead it was the police station.

"Summer?"

It was Jerry and I hesitated for a moment.

"Are you there?" he asked.

"Yes, Jerry. I'm here. What do you want?"

"I'm calling in an official capacity. The chief wants to elicit your help on this case."

"I can't help you."

"Please, Summer. We're completely stumped here. There are no clues and the witnesses aren't helping at all. The distraught parents of these kids have been calling and visiting the station. It's a bloomin' mess down here."

When he stopped speaking I could hear crying and shouting in the background. "Did you hypnotize the witnesses?" I finally asked.

There was silence. When he spoke a moment later it seemed to me that he was trying to control his temper. "Not yet. We were hoping you could talk with them, you know, try and ferret out anything we might have missed."

"I'll come down, but I'm telling you, I—" and then I remembered my visitation from the night before.

"What is it, Summer?"

"Something happened last night, but—"

"Was it a ghost? What did he or she tell you?"

"That's the thing—I couldn't hear what she was saying."

"Come down early tomorrow." The phone went dead after this command and I stared at it in frustration. Another morning where I'd be late to work and piss off my clientele, as well as wasting the police's time. Unless the ghost decided to speak up I had no clue what she was trying to get across.

That night I lay in bed with my eyes wide open, afraid to go to sleep for fear of what might wake me in the night. But then again, the ghost the night before had arrived unbidden in my living room. She had not appeared in a dream or a vision. Even Cutty had recognized her existence.

Sometimes I cursed this ability of mine to see ghosts. On our last case it had nearly got me killed. I also blamed my break-up with Jerry on the fall-out caused by that dip into the occult. Jerry had seemed to fall over a cliff after a maniac captured me and left me inside an air-proof room to die. And when I appeared to Jerry through the ether and told him where to find me, it was too much for his rational brain to take in. I knew his breakdown was not only due to that, but also his inability to apprehend the killer and the feeling of inadequacy that followed. Jerry was a proud man and didn't take well to being outdone by the likes of me—a lowly woman and an amateur sleuth. Jerry's father had died the year before, and that event coupled with what went down in Watch Hill had certainly sent him careening over the edge. I figured it had taken several weeks before he was back on duty.

As I drifted into sleep I saw myself with Jerry as we had been before all that happened—our easy life together, our nights of pure bliss. And then I was dreaming.

"Summer, where are you?"

I looked up and into Jerry's handsome face and felt his arms come around me, lifting me and pressing my body against his wide chest. When he kissed me I kissed him back, feeling everything I always felt when we were together.

"Why aren't we together?" I asked him.

He pulled back, his eyes turning dark. "You are keeping us apart," he told me.

A second later I was alone and then I woke with a start. Cutty was sitting on the bed, his gaze toward the open bedroom door. I heard Mischief, my black cat, give a yowl and a second later I was up and slinking toward the living room.

She was standing there again, her eyes on mine, but this time her hair was tangled and seemed filled with sticks and bits of bark, as though she'd been running through the forest. Mischief was attempting to rub on her legs but there was nothing there to rub against. He stared at me looking incensed and then stalked away as though it was all my fault.

"What is it?" I asked her. "What do you need to tell me?"

She pointed to the trashcan where I'd thrown the newspaper. "Please," she mouthed.

I moved to the trashcan and pulled it out, opening it to the headlines. "What do you know about this?" I asked, holding it open.

She read the headline and then buried her face in her hands. When she looked up again she shook her head. "You must—" she mouthed before she turned to look at something behind her. Her eyes went wide with fear and a second later she was gone.

This time instead of waiting around for her to reappear I went back to bed. But the sleep I got was minimal, my dreams filled with images of the children, their ghosts rising from their bodies and staring at me accusingly. When I finally woke in the morning I felt as though I'd never slept.

4

I thought about the ghost as I dressed and made coffee, wondering about what she hadn't said. And what could possibly scare a person who was already dead?

Since I did not own a car I reluctantly texted Jerry to see if he would give me a lift to the station. He texted back saying he'd swing by on his way to work. When he pulled up at my door in the squad car I wondered what my neighbors might think. It had been a long time since the last cop car debacle, the sirens blazing as Jerry took Nathan away from my house in handcuffs. Nathan, the man who'd stuck me in that box and killed our murder victim, had been about to do the same to me. If it hadn't been for Jerry—but that was then and this was now, I told myself sternly. Jerry had not bothered to call in all the months since then.

I hurried out the door, pulled it securely closed and then moved to the passenger side and climbed in. I gazed at my former boyfriend, surprised by his shoulder length hair, the heavy beard he sported. His eyes held a haunted expression. I felt nervous sitting next to him as though what lay between us hung in the air, creating a physical presence. "That's a new look for you. What does the chief think of it?" I asked, trying for a light tone.

Jerry smirked and gazed at me for a quick moment before looking away again. He put his foot on the gas. "She isn't too happy about it, but she's putting up with it for now. Since I'm going undercover so much she figures it's okay for the time being."

"Undercover? When did that start? I wouldn't think Ames had much call for that."

Jerry turned. "There's more going on in Ames than you'd think, Summer. We have several drug rings operating out in the country—meth labs and crack. Heroin is on the rise. And this last shooting proves that things are turning dangerous."

I felt a chill. "Do you think the shooter lives here?"

Jerry shrugged, stopping for a stop sign. When he put his foot on the gas again he had a frown on his face. "I'm hoping you can help with that. So far we have little to go on."

"I don't know what I can do. I'm not psychic like that. I can only help when a ghost tells me stuff, like Yvonne in our last case, and it seems that whoever did this is not a ghost." Jerry winced at the mention of Yvonne and I wished I hadn't said anything. "What does Sam say?"

"He's as stumped as the rest of us. I'm telling you the station has turned into a mental ward with parents screaming for revenge and no one to give them any good news."

"Do you have a grief counselor you can call in?"

"We've done that. What we need now is closure. I'm hoping you can help with that."

"Jerry, I…"

Jerry held up his hand as he turned into the police station parking lot. "Just talk with the witnesses, okay?"

I nodded and when he got out of the car I followed him into the station. There were several sets of parents in the lobby, half of them crying, the other half yelling at the officer in charge. It was utter chaos. Jerry opened the door into a private office and herded me inside.

"Summer, I'm glad you're here." Chief Sandra Marshall, a stocky woman in her fifties, shook my hand. "As you can see we have a situation on our hands. The witnesses haven't been able to tell us much of anything yet. I thought since you had some expertise in this area, you could…"

"I can try but I don't promise anything. I'm not a hypnotist."

She sighed and slanted a glance toward Jerry. "Take her into interrogation room one," she told him before heading out to field the uproar going on at the front desk.

Jerry left me in a windowless room that smelled of nervous sweat, where three women were seated at a metal table. I knew Mary Cozins since she often came into my store, and Heidi Markham was also familiar to me. Maggie Johnson was a churchgoer and so we didn't often cross paths, but I knew her face. Ames was a small town.

After talking with them for a few minutes I decided to do a guided visualization, leading them back to the moment of the shooting, but all it produced was tears on their part as they relived the horrible massacre. And worse than that it painted a clear picture in my mind of the mayhem, making me much more aware of what the teachers and children went through.

"I'm sorry!" Mary said, her face in her hands. "It's like the murderer put a spell on us!" She turned to Heidi. "Can you see him at all?"

Heidi shook her head, brown curls bouncing. "I don't even know if it was a him—it's like the memory is a blur. I swear it looked to me like another person was there, but the second form was hazy and indistinct. All I remember is brown hair, or maybe it was gray?"

When I turned to Maggie she was frowning, her arm

caught up in a sling from where a bullet had grazed her. "It was the devil—he put up a haze so we couldn't identify him." She looked to me for corroboration.

I shrugged. "Did it happen really fast?"

Heidi looked at Mary and then they both turned to me with tears in their eyes. "I don't know," Mary answered. She put her hands over her face and I could hear her sniffing.

"Do you remember the gun?"

"Big?" Mary said, glancing at Heidi.

Heidi shrugged. "All I can remember is how loud it was and how the sound seemed to go on and on." She stared into space. "There was something—like the shooter was fighting another person off, or—" she shook her head. "But there wasn't anybody else there."

Maggie stared at her. "I'm sure that was the devil. He can change his form and his face, you know."

No one responded to that and a few minutes later I thanked them and left the interrogation room. When the chief saw me she motioned me into her office. "What did you find out?"

"Did you know the school was a recruitment office during the Second World War?"

"Really?"

"I know you don't necessarily believe in this stuff, but I've had a visit from a ghost and I'm pretty sure it's Sadie Cumberland. She lost her husband and her son to that war. She keeps saying something like, *you've got to help her*, but I don't know who she's talking about."

Sandra frowned and pulled her fingers through her short brown curls. "And?"

"Sadie's granddaughter, Sarah, came into the store the other day—that's how I knew about Sadie."

"Sarah Cumberland. I'll have to bring her in for

questioning."

"She wouldn't be a suspect, though."

"No. I just want to talk with her about the building and anything she might know. At this point I feel like I have to follow every lead there is." She looked up and smiled. "Thanks, Summer. We'll call if we need anything else."

I left her office and went to find Jerry who was taking down notes from someone who I suspected was talking about another case. When he saw me he came over.

"Well?"

"Nothing. As I said, I think you need to hire a hypnotist."

Jerry shrugged. "The chief was hoping the station wouldn't have to shell out cash for this."

Ah ha, I thought to myself. I could just hear Jerry saying, *'Ask Summer, she'll do it for free.'*

"Can you give me a ride to the shop?"

Jerry looked over at Sandra and raised his eyebrows in some sort of non-verbal communication. The chief waved her hand as though giving him permission before turning back to the distraught parents.

"What do you think happened at the school?" I asked him once we were in the car.

"I think one of these meth-heads I was living with did it."

"Living with? What are you talking about?"

"I was embedded with these guys for nearly two months, but the chief pulled me out a week ago. I was pretty sure I'd been made and she was worried I'd get killed if I stayed. I never met the dude who runs the show, but they're all hopped up and crazy. I wouldn't put it past any one of them."

I stared into his sunken eyes, his long messy hair. "You look like hell you know. Are you doing drugs?"

Jerry glanced at me and then pressed down hard on the gas, throwing me back against the seat. He roared down the street, screeching to a halt across the street from Tarot and Tea. "Only pot," he answered, his gaze in the distance. "I had to do something to get them to trust me."

When his eyes met mine I noticed how bloodshot they were. "That gig seems kind of dangerous," I ventured.

"Yeah, well—that's the way it goes when you're a cop," he answered, one hand waving dismissively. "All I have to do now is arrest the bastards." He glanced out the window. "Looks like your clients are getting impatient."

I followed his gaze to the line of people waiting at my door. "Oh crap. Thanks for the ride," I said, hopping out and hurrying across the street. He zoomed away without a wave or a goodbye. Jerry had been into drugs when he was younger and having this kind of temptation seemed like asking for trouble.

I was headed into the back room to feed Tabby when I heard Mrs. Browning say, "I see you're with that handsome policeman again."

I stopped in mid-stride. "We aren't together—he took me down to the station this morning to talk with the witnesses, but it didn't do any good."

Mrs. Browning's eyes went wide. "Oh dear. This is such a blight on Ames—what those poor parents must be going through."

I nodded. "It's strange to me that no one remembers the shooter."

"That is odd. I wonder—" she said. But she didn't

finish her sentence when another customer walked by.

I continued into the back room and fed my kitty, scratching her behind the ears for a moment before heading into the store again. Mrs. Browning was notorious for not saying what was on her mind. I was sure she knew something, but trying to pry it out of her would not be an easy task.

Lack of customers led me to lock up early, glad to be finished for the day. My cottage was only two miles from Tarot and Tea and the walk home gave me a chance to come down from the stress of the day. But this evening things felt different. The trees seemed to bend toward me as I made my way along, the wind making an eerie whistling sound as it traveled through the mostly bare branches. I felt a prickling sensation on the back of my neck, and jumped when a car backfired. My nerves felt like the ends of an unraveling sweater and tension crept up my spine like some creepy crawly insect. Maybe it was the ghost from the night before, or maybe it was the strange wind and the clouds that were piling in, one on top of the other. Or maybe it was the image I now had in my mind of the shooting. I could see the shooter and the struggle going on between him or her and some other form that didn't seem corporeal. A ghost? Was this clairvoyance or my overactive imagination?

I hurried down the street and headed into Ames Market, glad to see the lights on and normal customers pushing shopping carts down the aisles. The spring flowers were still outside, but Joey, the manager, was moving them in off the street. I looked up at the dark sky, hoping it wouldn't start raining before I reached home. The owner, Pauline Ames, was already gone for the day. I knew the older woman had had some health issues recently and I hoped she was doing okay.

At the butcher counter Mr. Riddle greeted me. "Haven't seen you in a while, young lady. Are you keeping well?"

"Yes, Mr. Riddle. Thanks for asking. Can you cut me a small filet off that hunk of salmon?"

The older man smiled, showing ultra-white capped teeth. "Yes, indeed. How about that shooting?" he began, pulling the fish out to cut it. "Pretty nasty business for this town, wouldn't you say? People are afraid to go outside. Some think it was a satanic cult that did it."

This was a god-fearing town, but a satanic cult? That seemed over-the-top, even for Ames. I nodded, not wanting to get into it. I waited as he wrapped my fish and then took the package. But as I turned to go he said, "Are you still seeing that detective? What does he say?"

I shook my head. "He doesn't know. It's a real mystery." I hurried away before he could ask me any more questions, feeling the need to be at home with my dog and my cat with a glass of wine in my hand. Living in a small town made anonymity impossible. And if people were talking about satanic cults I hated to think what might come up next.

5

I was caught in a dream when I felt Cutty lick my face. When I opened my eyes he whined and then jumped off the bed. "What is it, little guy?" I asked, following him into the living room.

My ghost was standing there, her eyes wide with despair. "You must help her," she mouthed.

"Help who?" But she was already dissipating and a second later she was gone. It was pouring rain and I went to close the window in the kitchen, noticing my computer blinking. When I hit my mouse it came on, a message flashing in my e-mail. *"Just so you know, Sandra organized for a hypnotist."*

It was signed Jerry.

I hit reply and wrote, *"A ghost visited me again tonight. I think she's Sadie Cumberland who lost her husband and her son to the war. She asked me to help someone, but I don't know who she's referring to. Call me when you get a chance."*

I hit send and then wished I hadn't. Jerry was still shell-shocked from our last case that involved a ghost. This would not go over well. It was the biggest reason we weren't together now. And the way he'd acted in the car earlier hadn't helped either, with his clipped answers to my questions, and obvious anger about something he wasn't saying.

In bed I listened to the wind and rain lashing against my windows, wondering if the glass would loosen and break. My windows all needed to be re-puttied and I hadn't gotten around to it. I heard a couple of branches hit my roof and wondered if I should go out and check, but it was close to freezing outside and I was also too sleepy. I thought of the nighttime storm Jerry and I had gone through together a year ago, and how he'd gone out to check on my roof and come back soaking wet. After that we'd spent the night snuggled together in my bed. I pushed the memory away and closed my eyes.

By morning the storm had passed through, the sky a pale milky blue with wispy clouds still moving fast. I made coffee and fed Cutty and Mischief before checking my computer. There was a return message from Jerry that said. *Can I come by tonight? I need to talk to you about something.*

Talk to me about something? Was this regarding the case or something else? I pondered that while I thought about my answer, finally writing, *Sure. What time*? I pressed the send button and sat back, wondering if I would hear from him. He'd sent the other one late the night before. A second later my computer dinged in a message. *Six-thirtyish,* he wrote.

Okay, see you then, I answered before turning off my computer. I went to get a light jacket and headed out the door, locking it behind me. When I checked on the roof I saw a few branches stuck in my gutters but nothing that looked like damage.

The air was crisp and fresh after the storm and as I walked down the sidewalk toward the other side of town I lifted my face to the early morning sun. There wasn't much traffic this early and the few people I did see seemed distracted, with frowns on their faces as they hurried along looking down. When I heard a car pull up behind me I turned in time to see Becky, my friend who owned Daily Bread, rolling down the passenger side window. "Want a lift?"

I climbed into her ancient Honda Accord. Becky looked upset, her hair pulled back in an untidy ponytail. "You're late today," I said.

She shook her head, making her ponytail swing. "I was up half the night with Catherine Simpson. She lost her seven-year-old boy in the shooting."

"I'm so sorry! She's divorced, right?"

Becky nodded, navigating around some downed branches. "Her ex-husband blames her for the entire thing. She's an utter mess."

"That's ridiculous. How can it be her fault?"

"He's a jerk and always been—uses whatever he can to make her feel bad—as if she isn't feeling bad enough."

"No kidding. I talked to the witnesses yesterday and none of them can remember anything about the person who did this. Maggie Johnson seems to think it was the work of the devil."

Becky looked over at me, her blue eyes wide. "Maggie worries a lot about the devil. I've tried to dissuade her from this dark way of seeing the world but she hears this stuff at church—the minister preaches from the Old Testament. I wonder if there's witchcraft involved."

"Isn't that as bad as saying the devil did it? From the descriptions it almost seems like it was a ghost, but how could a ghost do it?"

Becky stared at the road, her eyes narrowed. "Douglas could."

"But he would never—"

Becky turned. "I know, I was just saying that if he could manage it, then maybe—"

"Good luck convincing the police of such a thing." A second later Becky pulled up to the curb across from my store. I opened the door. "Thanks for the ride."

"Are you coming to the full moon meeting? We're having a healing for the children and teachers who were killed and several of the parents will be there."

Our coven met every full moon at a large level spot out by the Ames River. It was the only time I had a chance of seeing my mother—however briefly. "When is it? I have no idea what phase we're in, and with all the rain I just figured it wouldn't happen."

"It's tomorrow night, and according to the weather channel it's supposed to be clear. But wear a heavy coat. It's going to be a special one since we'll have several new members joining us."

"I'll try, Becky."

Becky frowned. "Don't *try* Summer—be there!"

I laughed. "Okay." I slammed the car door and watched her weave her way down the street filled with broken limbs and trash. Several garbage cans were rolling around in the middle of the road and I went to replace them on the curb before heading across the street to Tarot and Tea.

It was close to noon when the woman who resembled my ghost came into the store. She looked exhausted with dark circles under eyes, her freckles standing out from skin as pale as ashes. I noticed for the first time the gray hair at her roots, the sort of burned look to her dyed brown hair. When she came up to the desk with a bottle of frankincense essential oil I said, "You seem so familiar. Have we met before the other day?"

She smiled wanly. "I'm Sarah Cumberland. I've been told I look just like my grandmother, Sadie. You might have seen her picture somewhere, like maybe at the school? She taught there and also worked there when it was first turned into the recruitment office."

I nodded and took her money, ringing her up. "Did you lose anyone in the shooting?" I asked, gently.

She started, her eyes round with what seemed like fear. "I knew several teachers there. It's a terrible tragedy." And after that statement she turned and hurried out the door.

I watched her go, wondering about her reaction to my question. Sarah had to be the person my ghost wanted me to help.

After she left I went into the back and made myself a sandwich from the sliced chicken, bread and lettuce I had left in my tiny refrigerator. When I came into the store a few minutes later a strange man was wandering around. I moved behind the desk and opened my store computer, checking on my inventory and at the same time trying to see what the guy was doing. I didn't have too many men as customers and this one was definitely a stranger in town.

He came up to the desk a few minutes later holding a bottle of clary sage oil. "I hoped you had a vapor machine."

He was young but looked ravaged, as though hit hard by life, his skin grayish and several teeth missing. "No. I only sell the infusers for the essential oils. Not sure if you can find a vaporizer here in Ames—it's kind of behind the times." I smiled.

He didn't smile back as he handed me some greasy bills from his stained and torn jacket pocket. I took the money, reminding myself to wash my hands as soon as he left. I could definitely picture him with an assault rifle in his hands mowing down those kids. And his stringy hair was brown.

Between Douglas and his essential oils and several older women from the assisted living apartments across from the Ames Market, I made good sales. I often wondered what Douglas did with his ongoing purchases of oils. Perhaps he had a woman friend and used them for massage. He was very elegant and had a way with the ladies. Now that I knew him, it was odd to think of him as a ghost.

At five I left the store, my mind occupied with taking a shower and dressing for Jerry's arrival. It didn't please me that I was already planning an outfit that I knew he'd like and going over some fabricated conversation that culminated with him kissing me. I shook myself mentally, moving my attention to the maple and oak limbs moving in the breeze, the whisper of wind that I could almost see. I was the only person on the sidewalk, and the large yards from which I normally heard kids laughter, were empty, the park as well. The weather was good for a change, and warm enough for shirtsleeves. It gave me an eerie feeling.

Cutty greeted me at the door, jumping into my arms as soon as I got inside. "What's with you?" I asked him, giving him a kiss on the top of his fuzzy head, but he didn't answer, only looked up soulfully. I put him on the floor and headed into the bathroom to take a shower.

I was still primping in front of the mirror when I heard Jerry's motorcycle. The Indian he'd bought the year before had a distinctive sound to its engine. Butterflies flitted through my stomach as I took one last look in the mirror, glad I'd taken the time to blow-dry my hair and apply a bit of lipstick. I had chosen a long sleeved V-necked black t-shirt over a pair of tight jeans. My worn cowboy boots completed the outfit I knew Jerry favored.

He had his hand out to knock when I opened the door. "Hi," I said, moving to let him in. We were almost the same height now that I was wearing my boots, his shoulder brushing mine as he went by. When I closed the door he was still standing there looking uneasy.

"Sit," I said, gesturing to the loveseat we'd bought together the previous summer.

"Got a beer?" he asked, dropping onto the couch and stretching his legs out.

I went to the kitchen and poured myself a glass of wine before reaching for the Dos Equis amber I knew he liked. I carried both into the living room, handed him his beer, and then sat across from him on the chair. "What's up?"

Jerry took a long pull from his bottle and stared at the floor. "This case is a bitch," he muttered. "This day has been pure hell."

"What about the meth case? Are you still working it?"

Jerry shook his head. "We need to get a team out there and arrest those jokers but since the shooting everything else has taken a back seat. You would not believe what's going on—it's like the entire town has lost its collective mind." He looked up. "But that isn't why I'm here."

"Before you start whatever it is, I have to tell you that some strange guy came into the store today asking for a vaporizer—I assume for marijuana. He looked beat-up, Jerry. Is he one of the guys you were living with?"

"What did he look like?"

"Brown hair, bad teeth, filthy clothes."

Jerry let out a snort. "That could be any one of them. They're all meth heads—bad teeth go along with it."

"He was tall with brown hair and I think his eyes were hazel, although they were so bloodshot I couldn't tell."

"Could be Cable. He's into pot. Why do you care?"

"He could be the shooter."

Jerry raised his eyebrows. "Well, that's true enough. I wish the chief would send us out there. For some reason she blows me off when I try and link the drug ring and the shooting."

I stared at his dirty ripped jeans, his ancient hiking boots, picking up the smell of sweat, dirty hair and the miasma of pot. For some reason it didn't turn me off. "You look like you're one of them, Jerry."

Jerry scoffed. "This is my persona, Summer."

"Even though you're not embedded with them anymore? How long did you say it's been?"

"A week. It takes a while to come out of character."

I tried to detect some hint of humor in his tone but he was frowning and looked belligerent. A moment went by and then another with Jerry staring toward the dark window. By now I'd turned on a couple of lamps. "Another beer?" I finally asked.

He nodded and held out the empty bottle. When I got back from the kitchen he'd removed his boots and was leaning against the pillow on one end, his feet on the other arm, a position he'd taken often when we lived together. "Please, make yourself comfortable," I said.

"Listen, Summer. The only reason I came over tonight is because my therapist thinks I need closure."

I felt a pain below my ribs. "Your therapist asked you to talk to me?"

"That's right. I even argued with her about it."

"And how are you supposed to get closure?"

Jerry swung his legs off the couch and leaned forward. "How do I know? I guess I need to tell you I'm sorry?"

I felt my face grow hot. "Sorry for what, exactly? Leaving me and never calling, or coming over tonight on false pretenses?"

Jerry frowned, staring at me. "What false pretenses? Did you think we were getting back together?"

I stood up, nearly spilling my wine. "Get out," I said, pointing to the door.

"Why do I need to go?"

"Because I don't want you in my house. Because you're an ass, and because I don't like you right now."

Jerry looked bewildered as he rose from the couch. He pulled on his boots and laced them up, his eyes on the floor. "I was supposed to talk to you about what happened, Summer."

"Well, you didn't. Tell your therapist that you failed your homework. You can also tell her for me that she's doing a shitty job." I headed to the door and opened it.

Jerry didn't meet my eyes as he walked past me out the door. I slammed it shut behind him, locked it, and then burst into tears.

It took me nearly an hour to get control of myself. Cutty didn't like my state of mind and whined and hung out beside me on the chair where I huddled, my legs pulled up to my chin. Finally I let out a long sigh and headed into the kitchen to find something to eat. When my phone rang I ignored it, assuming it was Jerry again, trying to make up for his asinine behavior.

After eating a sandwich I poured another glass of wine and checked my phone. The missed call was Agnes and I hit her name on my favorites list.

"Summer, can you come over for dinner tomorrow night?"

I hesitated, thinking there was some conflict, but nothing came to mind. "Sure. Would you like me to bring anything?"

"No. Sam's cooking a casserole of some sort and we have plenty of wine. Around six? Sam will come and get you."

I agreed and hung up the phone without telling her about Jerry. It would only have her worrying about her wedding again.

By the time I'd checked my computer for messages, searched on Facebook for things to comment on, and looked up any news regarding the shooting, it was nearly eleven. When I reached the bedroom Cutty was already curled into a tight ball next to my pillow. I undressed and crawled in beside him, hugging him close as I felt tears well again. I am not going to cry, I told myself sternly. Jerry and I are through and that's that. But a part of me didn't buy it, despite his behavior.

I woke with a start at 2:00 a.m. Cutty was staring at a blue glow coming from the living room, his eyes wide. Had I left my computer on? I climbed out from under my down comforter and padded after my dog, not surprised when I saw Sadie Cumberland standing in the middle of my living room. She looked a bit more filled in this time, her eyes pleading as she watched me approach. "They questioned her," she said in a clear voice. "You have to help her."

"Are you talking about Sarah?" I asked, but she evaporated into thin air before she could tell me more.

This had to be about her granddaughter—who else would she be worried about? But why in the world would the police suspect Sarah?

6

I was heading home from Tarot and Tea the next afternoon when I realized what the conflict about dinner was. Tonight was full moon with no cloud cover—the perfect coven night. It was too late to do anything without being rude and upsetting Agnes and Sam.

A dark semi-clean skirt was lying crumpled on my closet floor and I slipped it on. I pulled a light wool sweater over my head and then braided my hair into one braid and pulled it over one shoulder. When I checked myself out in the mirror I realized the skirt needed to be ironed but there wasn't enough time. I figured my very cool black leather boots made up for it. As I was applying lipstick I noticed the hollow expression in my eyes. Damn Jerry!

With the clear air the temperature had dropped and I threw on my down coat to wait for Sam. When he drove up I hopped into the passenger side. "Thanks for picking me up," I said.

Sam smiled, his blue eyes crinkling at the corners. "No problemo." He pulled away from the curb and drove unhurriedly toward the newer neighborhoods where Agnes and he lived. "Did Agnes tell you she found a dress?" he asked, turning.

"No, we didn't talk very long. Do you like it?"

Sam shrugged. "I'm not allowed to see it until the wedding—bad luck."

I grinned. "That superstition is only about the day of the wedding, Sam."

"Really? Get her to try it on tonight, would you? I'd like to pick a tux and a *boutonnière* that matches."

I hadn't liked Sam very much when I first met him, but he'd softened since he and Agnes had been together. "You are such a romantic. I never would have guessed it."

Sam chuckled. "Agnes brings it out in me. I owe it all to you."

"Me? All I did was introduce you. Speaking of introductions, do you know Sarah Cumberland?"

Sam frowned. "Why do you ask?"

"She was in the store and she seemed kind of nervous. Is she related to any of the teachers or the kids that were killed?"

Sam grimaced, his mouth making a thin line. "I shouldn't tell you this, but Sarah Cumberland is on our suspect list."

"What? Why?"

"After you mentioned her to the chief she called her in. Her answers to the questions were a little off and so we got a warrant and searched her house. We found the murder weapon."

"That can't be right. She's really nice. She couldn't have done this."

"Maybe she went crazy for a moment, or maybe she's a sociopath. All I can tell you is she had a Thompson submachine gun in her house, and when we checked with ballistics we determined it was the one."

I stared out the window too shocked to say anything. That was what the ghost of Sadie Cumberland had been trying to tell me.

We arrived at the house a moment later and I was

very glad to leave the conversation. Agnes opened the door and grabbed my arm to pull me inside. "I didn't know whether you'd come," she whispered, glancing at Sam behind me.

"Why wouldn't I come?"

"Coven night," she hissed in my ear.

"I remembered it earlier today but it was too late. I was surprised you forgot."

Agnes motioned me into the living room and gestured to a chair. Sam was in the kitchen, checking his stew. "I didn't forget. I'm not going anymore," she told me. "It bothers Sam."

"Why should he care?"

Agnes shrugged. "He doesn't like to think about ghosts. It freaks him out."

"And what about Douglas, your father? He's a ghost."

Agnes smiled. "I'm not sure Sam believes that."

I shook my head. "He has to know. Sam was involved in the last case in Watch Hill with Yvonne's ghost. Maybe he doesn't want to think about it."

"Could be. But I want to keep him happy."

I stared at my freewheeling friend with the tattoos of goddesses up and down her arms. I didn't like her giving up a part of herself in order to please a man. "Sam says you have the dress. Can I see it?"

Agnes jumped up, her eyes bright. "It's in my closet."

I followed her into the darkened bedroom, waiting while she switched on a light. Her closet was neatly organized, each article of clothing folded neatly and stacked in piles on the shelves. I thought of my closet at home, shelves overflowing, and piles of clothing on the floor.

She pulled out a gray dress and held it up. It had long sleeves, the bodice covered in sequins and ending below the waist in a V. The underskirt was gray satin with a sheer overskirt that shimmered in the light and ended just above her ankles in four inches of lace. "Did you find this at Once Again?"

Agnes shook her head, her chin length dark hair swinging and then moving perfectly back into place. "I went to a vintage store in New York."

"It suits you perfectly—very twenties."

"I have a head piece to go with it," she said, pulling out a wide band of gray covered in sequins. "Do you think it's too much?"

I shook my head. "You'll look awesome. What am I going to wear?"

"Anything you like that goes with this. You look good in black."

"For a wedding?"

"The bridal magazines seem to think it's fine for the bridesmaids to wear black. And anyway, ours isn't very traditional since I'm not wearing white."

"I'll check in Once Again on Saturday. Will you come with me?"

"Sure, I'd love to." She put her delicate nose into the air and sniffed. "I think dinner's ready."

I followed her into the dining room, noticing how monochromatic and spare her style was. The furniture was Asian, dark and simple. Her walls had a few woodblock prints of birds and animals. The place was immaculate. "Are you going to sell this house once you're married?"

Agnes glanced at Sam who was wearing an apron and placing a casserole dish on the table. "Sam and I are planning to look for a house in the country. I want a couple of dogs and a big enough space for them to run."

Dogs? This was a new side of Agnes.

Sam grinned. "She's been worried about the mess they make, but she's found several breeds that don't shed."

"More than several," Agnes added, motioning for me to sit. "There's Airedales, Poodles, Puli, Brussels Griffon, Schnauzers, and Portuguese Water dog," she said, ticking them off with her fingers. "I'm leaning toward the Griffon."

"You have done some research," I said, reaching for the plate Sam had dished out for me.

Agnes smiled. "It's hard to not get one now, but I can't have a puppy underfoot with the wedding coming up and everything." She glanced at Sam.

"I heard that you and Jerry made up," Sam said, changing the subject.

"Made up? Hardly. He's been a real jerk." I glanced quickly at Agnes. "But don't worry, I can put up with him for one day."

"He told me he was dating someone and I assumed it was you," Sam said, looking down at his plate.

"Not bloody likely," I muttered.

We talked about the wedding and this and that for a while as we ate, and then I asked Sam, "Are you arresting Sarah or do you need more evidence?"

Sam glanced worriedly at Agnes before answering. "I don't know for sure. I know the chief told her to stick around town. It could happen this week, and as you know the parents' are screaming to have someone arrested. Jerry doesn't think she's the one, but the chief is ready to pin it on someone. The gun is kind of the clincher."

"Can we talk about something else?" Agnes said, her fork in midair. "You promised me, Sam."

She was pale, her dark eyes filled with unshed tears. "Sorry sweetheart," Sam said. "But this news should make you happy. It means there's an end to it."

Agnes stood abruptly, knocking over her chair in the process. "An end to it? How can you say that? Those parents will mourn their kids for the rest of their lives!" She turned and ran from the room and I heard the bedroom door slam shut.

I turned to Sam. "Why is this affecting her so much?"

Sam shrugged. "I wish I knew. She's been like this since the day it happened. Listen, Summer, I hate to do this—but could you take the bus home? I have to go to her."

"Can I at least help clean up?"

"No. Agnes won't be happy if I let you do that." Sam stood and headed toward the bedroom. "Give her a call tomorrow, would you? She needs your support."

I carried the plates to the sink and then went to get my coat. When I left the house the stars were out, billions of them in the dark dome above me. The moon was full tonight and just risen. I waited at the bus stop, wondering if it was time for me to buy a car. I still had a driver's license—I couldn't keep counting on my friends to take me everywhere. My mind turned from that topic to the coven. When I looked at my phone I realized it was barely nine, not too late to go. I searched for the numbers for the taxi company and when someone answered I asked them to pick me up at the bus stop on High Street.

The taxi dropped me off at another bus stop a mile from the path that led toward the river. We were more than five miles away from town in an uninhabited stretch of land that had formerly been used to grow alfalfa and soybeans. When I handed over my money he looked worried. "Are you sure you'll be all right? I don't think the busses are running this late and there's nothing out here."

I smiled reassuringly. "A friend is picking me up. I'll be fine."

After he drove off I climbed the wall behind me and headed toward the low hill that rose up behind the bus stop. It took me nearly forty minutes to reach the familiar path that led to the river. When I looked at my phone I had no cell signal but I could still read the time. It was nearly eleven, the hour when coven members began to congregate. I had a moment of excitement, thinking about my mother and what I wanted to say to her. She had not been here the last time I'd attended. I stopped to watch the moon, luminous and seeming so close, a feeling of contentment filling in the hollow place I'd grown used to. When I turned back to the path I ran into Becky who gave me a quick hug, her smile of welcome making me glad I'd come.

"Didn't know if you'd make it or not. Where's Agnes?"

"Having an emotional breakdown. I had dinner there but Sam made the mistake of bringing up the shooting and Agnes lost it."

"Too bad she didn't come. This meeting would have helped her."

When Becky and I arrived at the clearing a large crowd had already gathered. I saw many new faces, some with tears shining on their cheeks. My mother was there and I hurried over to say hello.

"My darling girl, I'm so glad you're here," she whispered, giving me a hug. "I know you've been struggling with the shooting but don't let it take over your life. All will be well in the end."

I was about to ask her about Sarah and the shooting and how to help her when the grand master, Byron Forsyth, appeared in the center, standing on a stone that had been placed there years before. He wore dark robes, his rugged features in shadow. "We are gathered here tonight to release the souls who are still in pain," he said in a sonorous tone. His gaze traveled the circle before he began to chant, his arms held up in supplication to the bright orb above us. *"Oh goddess moon we feel your magic, we bow to you and take in your power to use only for good."*

Everyone repeated the chant, the sound growing and swelling. Candles were lit within the group and passed around so that each person held one. When a woman joined Byron I recognized Marguerite Powers, her long robes swaying as she moved to his side. She looked powerful and beautiful, much younger than I remembered, her eyes shining in the moonlight. They stood in front of each other for a long moment before moving together, their kiss a symbol of the melding of the male and female energies and cementing the union of the two.

I had a quick flash of how this was done in the olden days, the carefully selected man and woman stripped of clothing, the ritual mating in front of the gathered crowd that could lead to offspring who would carry on the traditions— animal sacrifices made to the gods and goddesses of old. The metaphors were ancient, our sexuality connecting us to the animal world and as natural as breathing—the ritual sacrifices to ensure life. But here in the modern world these darker traditions had been abandoned. I chuckled to myself, trying to imagine

Byron and Marguerite with gooseflesh rising on their wrinkled skin as they lay naked on the cold stone, their aging limbs entwined.

They moved apart and each picked up a bowl filled with rose water, which they sprinkled as they walked in opposite directions, meeting on the other side. *"Who wishes to be the one?"* they called out together, the male and female voices merging in a symphony of sound. I knew that this meant the symbolic representation of the children killed. Before I could think what I was doing I had stepped forward and into the center of the circle.

"Summer McCloud, are you willing to feel the pain of death and heal all that has been lost?"

I nodded, letting them anoint me with rose water, their dark robes swishing against me. I closed my eyes feeling the energies swirl around and through me, making me dizzy. A collective roar began and the crowd moved closer and closer until I could feel their hot breath on my face. A searing pain began in my feet and moved upward, encasing my entire body in agony. I let out a piercing shriek and fell to my knees. Hands were on me, moving in soothing motions. I heard the chant begin, the swell as it rose in volume. *"Oh goddess moon, Let this child go!"* I heard Byron shout. These words were echoed over and over as everyone repeated the words. I was huddled on the ground now the pain so excruciating that I wondered if I would recover. Why had I volunteered for this? But as soon as I thought I would die of the pain it was gone. *"Rise child and know that you are released! Blessed be!"*

I opened my eyes and pushed myself up, my body light. I thought for one moment that I might float upwards with the ghosts of the children and teachers, moving into the pellucid moonlight that sent shafts of brilliance down on our group. But my feet were firmly planted on the earth. And then every single person there hugged me. And when that was over they hugged each other, no one escaping the comfort of caring arms. All had tears in their eyes, their faces awash in grief—but under it I could see the release that had come from what had been done here. And then the ceremony was over.

The crowd dispersed, my mother disappearing before I could get a chance to talk with her. Clusters of people moved away up the path. I saw Byron and Marguerite, their ceremonial robes gone revealing casual clothes, belying what had taken place. When Becky touched my arm I started, still caught up in the memory of what had happened.

"Are you okay?" she asked me worriedly.

I nodded, unable to speak for a moment. "It hurt, Becky. How did they make it hurt like that?"

Becky gazed at me, her eyes dark. "They didn't make anything happen, Summer. It was the energies, the power we conjured. This was the most powerful meeting I've ever attended. I was worried about you. At one point I—"

"Thought I might die? So did I." I tried to smile but tears came into my eyes. "I saw them, Becky. I saw each one of those children and Linda and Mary. I felt the physical pain, the fear and the moment of death. But at the end they were smiling. I wish Agnes had been here."

Becky nodded. "We all saw them, Summer. I'll give you a lift home."

It was two in the morning before I got into bed, my mind whirling with the images of the night. I'd been going to the coven meetings for several years but I'd never experienced anything like what I'd experienced tonight. And why I'd walked into that circle was beyond my understanding. I certainly hadn't intended to.

7

The next morning I used a lull in the store to look through online dating sites, wondering if this was what I would have to stoop to. I really needed a date for the wedding, since I was sure Jerry would have one—I couldn't go there alone and see him with another woman on his arm. I had to accept that Jerry was not available, and even if he had been I didn't want him. I was still furious about our last meeting.

I called Agnes around eleven to see how she was and tell her about the meeting.

"I'm fine now. Sam calmed me down. He promised me he wouldn't talk about the case, and yet there he was, holding forth."

"It was my fault," I said. "I was the one who asked about it."

"Whatever. Let's just drop it. Thanks for calling."

I was just about to tell her about the meeting when I realized she'd hung up. What had gotten into her? And why was the shooting so personal to her? I turned off my computer as Douglas arrived.

"Have you seen my daughter?" he asked.

"I had dinner with her before the meeting last night—why?"

"She's been avoiding me since I spoke to her about the shooting and her wedding."

"That's odd. She seems overly involved with it all— the shooting, I mean. Do you have any idea why that would be?"

Douglas shook his head. "She's sensitive like her mother, but I'm not sure why this has thrown her so off balance."

"Was she close to any of those kids?"

"I don't know. She hasn't said anything to me if she was. Can you talk with her, Summer? I'm afraid this will affect the wedding plans."

"I won't let it," I said, patting his arm. "She's going to help me pick out a dress this weekend. Maybe we'll have a chance to talk then."

Douglas left shortly after that and I was alone in the store again. I began to wonder about my lack of customers. Was everyone staying home because they were afraid a homicidal maniac was roaming the streets? I thought about my walk home the day before and how I hadn't seen any children in the streets or in the yards or in the park. If this case didn't get solved soon the entire town would need therapy. I hoped what we'd done the night before would have an effect on things.

Just as I was closing up Sarah pushed open the door, her eyes red from crying. "They're going to arrest me," she whispered, looking around. "Are you friends with anyone down there? You have to help me."

"My detective friend, Sam, said they found the murder weapon at your house."

Sarah grabbed my arm. "That gun belonged to my grandfather. It's an antique and has always been locked in a case, ever since I can remember. My house belonged to my grandparents and my parents after them. I can't understand how the police could suspect me of doing such a terrible thing!"

"I believe you, but I'm not sure what I can do, Sarah. I'll talk with Sam, but I suggest you get a good lawyer."

Sarah began to cry. "If it's the weapon and I didn't do it, then who did? They'll never believe me!"

"Talk to a lawyer," I said, giving her a hug.

I felt shaken after she left, as though everyone I knew was being affected by the shooting. I hadn't had any more visits from my ghost, and she hadn't been at the coven meeting, but I wondered if I would tonight, especially since Sarah was now on the Ames most wanted list. Would they really arrest her? I had to talk to Sam or someone at the station and find out what in the world was going on.

I was on my way home, my mind a million miles away, when my cell phone rang. The caller I.D. was not one I knew but I answered anyway.

"Is this Summer McCloud?" a male voice asked.

"Yes, who is this?"

"This is Jim Salazar. I work at the Ames Gazette. I was wondering if I could interview you."

"Me? Why me?"

"From what I've heard you talk to ghosts," he said in a reasonable tone. "It's a story that could definitely increase our readership."

"Who told you this?"

"Jerry Brady is a friend of mine. He said you two lived together for a while."

"Yes, we did, but we're barely friends now. How did the topic of ghosts come up?"

"When we were at the Pig and Pint he told me he broke up with you because of what he termed, 'your extreme weirdness', and when I asked him what he meant he told me about your last case. I have to say I find it intriguing."

All of a sudden I wanted to bare my soul to this man, if for no other reason than to spite Jerry. He broke up with me because of my extreme weirdness? What a liar and coward! He walked away because of his own fragile ego, not because of me. "I'd be happy to talk with you, Jim. Where and when?"

We decided to meet at seven at the Pig and Pint. I couldn't wait to give him every tiny detail of my previous case with Jerry as well as the one I was working on now—well, working on, was a slight exaggeration, but I did feel that the ghost was keeping me informed.

I looked up when a car honked, realizing I was halfway across the street. The driver swerved to miss me and then yelled something unintelligible out the window—probably a swear word. I shook myself free of my reverie and hurried to my house.

The Pig and Pint was dark when I walked in, the only glow coming from the inset lights over the bar. I saw a man looking at me and when he stood I realized I'd seen him somewhere before. He was probably in his late thirties, tall and lean, like a runner. He nodded and came toward me smiling.

"Summer?" he said, taking me by the arm.

"Hi Jim. Have we met before?"

He shook his head. "I don't think so. I'd remember if we had." He lifted his brows as he looked me over. "I recognized you from Jerry's description. There aren't many women in town with hair the color of acorns."

My hand went up to smooth the wayward mop as he steered me toward a table in the back.

"What would you like to drink?" he asked, signaling for the waiter.

"White wine would be fine."

As he ordered I studied him, noticing his strong profile, the look of seriousness on his face. His physique was the complete opposite of Jerry's stocky build. When he turned his gaze on me I realized that his Latin heritage lent a seductive air, his dark eyes mysterious as he watched me.

"So, Summer, how long have you been able to talk to ghosts?" he asked placing his elbows on the table and leaning forward.

I laughed nervously. "I guess the first time was after Serena's murder. Do you know about that?"

Jim nodded, taking a pull from his beer. "I grilled Jerry for details about you before I decided to call."

"That was a couple of years ago, and since then I've…"

"Tell me about this latest case—did a ghost tell you Sarah was innocent?"

I stared at him, surprised. "Who told you that?"

Jim laughed. "I think it was Jerry. I have a way of getting people to open up to me. But seriously, Summer, a ghost? Don't you think it would be hard for the prosecution to swallow?" He leaned back and took a swig of his beer, a smile curling up the corners of his full mouth.

I nodded and took a drink from the glass of wine the waiter put down in front of me. "You're probably right. What I need to do is back that up with some real facts."

"Facts you don't have yet, I take it?"

"What exactly is your article going to focus on—a weirdo who talks with ghosts or a young woman who is different from other people and can connect with the beyond? Why are you asking questions about the case?"

He shook his head and glanced around the room. "Jerry said if it hadn't been for all that you two would still be together. Is that how you feel?"

When I met his gaze I was startled by the look in his eyes. Was he coming on to me? "Jerry and I—well, he went into a tailspin after the last case. That's the reason we're not together."

"So you still love him?"

"Are you planning to put this in your article?" I said clunking my glass down on the table and nearly spilling it.

Jim shrugged and turned his hands palms up. "To be perfectly frank I'd like to ask you out. Jerry told me I'd like you and he was right. The article was a ruse to meet you, I'm afraid. Sorry it you're offended, but I didn't know how else to go about it."

I smiled, gazing into his soulful eyes. "Yeah, I guess meeting people is getting harder and harder. I almost succumbed to a dating site."

Jim laughed. "You? I would have thought you had your pick of any guy around."

"Do you see a lot of available men in here, Jim?" I asked, gazing around at the couples and the much older men sitting at the bar.

He followed my gaze. "I see what you're talking about. So how about it—can I pick you up, say, tomorrow night at seven? I'll take you to Saffron and Seaweed, not to a place like this."

I frowned, contemplating a date with this man. He was good-looking but slick in a way that made me nervous. On the other hand I was attracted to him. "Are you really a reporter?"

He grinned. "I am a reporter and I would love to do an article about you. But let's get to know each other over dinner first, okay?"

"Okay, but only because I want a free dinner."

Jim laughed.

I hailed a taxi and when I was climbing inside I saw Jim standing in the doorway of the Pig and Pint with a broad smile on his face. I waved and then pulled out my cell phone and punched in Jerry's numbers. When he answered I said, "Why are you playing matchmaker? I don't need your help."

"What are you talking about?"

"You know exactly what I'm talking about. Jim Salazar."

"Who is Jim Salazar?"

I hit end and shoved the phone in my purse without answering his question.

"Is everything all right, lady?" the driver asked.

"Fine," I answered distractedly, my thoughts on Jerry and why he would tell Jim that we'd like each other. Why was he getting involved in my love life?

The next evening I dressed up for my date with Jim, pinning my hair on top of my head and wearing a wool dress that accented what few curves I had. I pulled on my black leather boots and then applied ruby lipstick. When I heard the knock on the door I took one last look in the mirror, noticing the flush in my cheeks and the sparkle in my eyes. This could be fun.

When we reached the restaurant Jim came around and opened my door and then offered his arm, leading the way inside the posh restaurant. This was only the second time I'd been here. He'd made a reservation and we were seated immediately at a table along the back wall. The space was lit with fairy lights, making it intimate and cozy.

After we ordered we chatted, mostly about the upcoming case and what I knew about it.

"So why do you think this Sarah Cumberland is innocent?" he finally asked. "I mean besides the ghost aspect."

"I just know. For one thing she's in her sixties and has no motive that I can determine."

"And yet the chief seems comfortable with her as a suspect?"

I shrugged and forked a piece of salmon into my mouth. "The chief is wrong."

Jim seemed to relax after this, leaning back in his chair and staring at me in a way that made me very nervous. "You look delectable tonight, Summer," he said. "Glad you agreed to have dinner with me. One more thing before we change the subject. Are you looking into any real evidence that might point away from the suspect?"

I shook my head. "Not so far but I hope to find something."

"What about her prints on the murder weapon—how can you still think she didn't do it?"

"I told you before—I just know."

"Okay, enough of that. Now tell me all about Summer McCloud—what do you like to do when you're not talking to ghosts?"

The rest of the evening went well, our banter turning to matters more personal. He told me he'd just come out of a bad relationship and that meeting me was helping his mood considerably. What was it about this guy that attracted me? He was not at all like Jerry or Tom in either build or personality, and yet he held me spellbound with his funny stories and his warm fingers on mine across the table.

By the time we left I was in his thrall, unable to keep my eyes off him. When we reached my house and he asked if he could come in I said yes, going against the little voice in my head that screamed no.

While I was bringing in the brandy Cutty ran into the living room growling in a way I had never heard before.

"Cutty! What's got into you? Stop it!" I put the glasses down and grabbed my dog and dragged him away. I shut him in the bedroom and by the time I got back to the living room Jim had removed his shoes and was leaning against the back of the loveseat, the brandy snifter in his hand. He patted the seat next to him. "Come sit by me," he said.

A frisson of nervousness moved through my body. I knew nothing about this man, had never met him before yesterday. For all I knew he could be a psychopath or the shooter grilling me to see what I knew.

"I think I'll stay over here," I said, picking up the glass of brandy on the coffee table and taking it with me to the chair across from him.

He frowned and leaned forward. "Are you afraid of me?"

"No. I'm just not ready for anything you might be thinking about."

"A mind reader?" He chuckled. "I'd like to say I don't have any lascivious thoughts, but that wouldn't be true." He took a long sip of his brandy and pointed to my, as yet untouched, glass. "Drink up, maybe you'll decide I'm not so bad after all."

I picked up my glass and took a sizable sip, feeling the heat of it as it slid down my throat.

"Good brandy, Summer. Did you get it locally?"

I nodded. "It's one my mother liked. I almost never drink it—it tastes good tonight."

Jim watched me take another long drink, his gaze sliding over me from head to toe as he raised his glass again. "Take another sip and tell me what it reminds you of," he said. "Can you taste the floral notes, the hint of coal?"

I laughed. "Hint of coal?" I took another swallow. "I wouldn't say coal—maybe diesel fumes?" I laughed again and felt a strange languor come over me. I wanted very badly to lie down but I knew Jim would take it as an invitation. I closed my eyes for a moment, resisting the urge to lie back against the chair. Why was I suddenly so tired? When I opened my eyes Jim was staring at me, his eyes bright.

"I'd like to take you to bed tonight. What do you say to that?"

"I'd say no, Jim." I put my glass down and stood up, realizing I was quite dizzy. "It's late and I think you should probably leave."

When he stood and moved toward me I backed up and nearly fell down. Jim was there less than a second later, his arms going around me. "I need to get you into bed," he murmured, his lips on my neck.

"You need to leave," I said feebly from within the circle of his arms. I felt paralyzed, unable to summon the strength to get him out of my house.

"Summer, I can tell you're attracted to me. Why not give in to it?" he muttered. "Let me help you into bed. You seem tired."

No—but the word did not reach my lips, only registering inside my brain. I felt him pick me up and carry me toward the bedroom but I was unable to resist. When we reached the bedroom door and he opened it, Cutty came bounding out, his snarls momentarily waking me out of my stupor.

"Jesus, you little shit!" Jim yelled. He kicked my dog, sending him careening across the wooden floor where he fell on his side and lay still.

The next time I became aware of things I was on my

bed, my dress pulled off my arms, my bra removed. Jim leaned over me his glittering eyes on my naked upper body. "Get out," I tried to yell, but it sounded like a whisper. And then I was falling into darkness even though I was still aware of my dress being removed, the feel of Jim's thumb as he hooked it into the elastic of my underpants. When I tried to lift my arm to stop him it felt like it weighed hundred pounds.

"You want me—I can see it in your eyes," he said. "Don't deny it."

I tried to struggle, to move away, but all I could do was lie there like a dead fish. I dimly noticed that he had no clothes on and was very ready to proceed with or without my permission. I wanted to scream, to kick him, anything to stop what I knew was about to happen, but I was unable to move.

I heard a sound in the back of my mind, a sort of click or bark, I wasn't sure. All I knew was that Jim paused and looked over his shoulder, giving me hope. He left me lying there and a moment later I was dimly aware of shouting and Jerry's voice raised in anger. I must have slept or passed out for a while because when I opened my eyes again Jerry was sitting on the bed next to me. "Are you all right?" he asked, his forehead creased in worry.

I managed to nod but that was all.

When I opened my eyes again Jerry was dozing in the chair next to the bed. Light was streaming through the window. When I turned to look at the clock, I was surprised to see it read 8:30. I tried to stand but my legs felt wobbly, and then Jerry was there, his arm around my waist. "Do you need to go to the bathroom?"

I gazed at the pajamas I was wearing—Jerry must

have dressed me. "I—I don't know. Yes, I think I do."

Jerry helped me into the bathroom and left me there, and when I came back out he was standing guard.

"How long have you been here? What happened—where's Jim?"

"Jim is behind bars, Summer, where he belongs. The guy drugged you, and if I hadn't happened by, he would have raped you."

A shiver went through me. "I felt like I was paralyzed—I couldn't move. Did he—?"

"That's what Rohypnol does. He put it in your brandy. And no, to answer your other question. I got here just in time. " He stared at me for a long moment with a concerned expression and then said, "I dropped by last night to talk to you about this Jim Salazar character—after you called I remembered the name—he works for the prosecutor's office. He's a PI. I had no idea you had a date with him."

"A PI? He told me he was a reporter. What did he want from me?"

"Maybe he was digging to see how much you knew about Sarah's defense. He was a fool to roofie you—his career is toast now."

A scene flew through my mind and I grabbed his arm. "Where's Cutty?"

Jerry smiled. "Cutty's fine. But I'll tell you what, he did not like that guy—he went nuts when I dragged Jim out of here."

"Jim kicked him—he's not hurt?"

"No." He pulled his fingers through his beard. "Listen, Summer—if you're feeling better I've got to get back to the station. I'll call you later, okay?"

8

It had been a week since the ordeal with Jim, and still the incident plagued me, nightmares interrupting my sleep and a sense of helplessness invading me. I had not heard from Jerry again. In some ways I was glad, since having him see me like that made me feel stupid for letting it happen as well as vulnerable. My friend Becky suggested I see a professional, telling me that an experience of this nature could linger and leave me with trust issues, but so far I hadn't done anything about it.

Since it was Saturday I was due at the store at ten instead of nine. I should have gone early since I had received a shipment of boxes that needed to be catalogued and unpacked, but I didn't have my normal enthusiasm. The day was already getting away from me since I'd decided to close at three to look for a bridesmaid dress with Agnes. We'd originally planned it for last weekend but Agnes had bugged out at the last minute claiming illness. And it was a good thing considering what had happened to me that Friday night. I shuddered as I relived the taste of the liquor and felt the sensation of paralysis. I was pretty sure I would never drink brandy again.

I left the house feeling somewhat alive after several cups of coffee, but my mood was as dark as the threatening sky. Halfway there the rain began and I cursed silently for not remembering my umbrella. By the time I reached the store I was drenched and shivering, my hand shaking as I fitted the key into the lock. When I pushed the door open I gasped in horror. Someone had come in and ransacked my store, the shelves of books overturned, essential oils in a pile of liquid and glass in the middle of the floor, the miasma of varied scents filling the air. The boxes I hadn't yet unpacked had been slashed, the contents joining the rest of the mess. "Kitty? Are you here?" But Tabby was fine, her hurried approach and purring soothing some of my frazzled nerves. I grabbed my phone and dialed the station. Of course it would be Jerry who answered the call.

"Leave everything as it is. I'll be right there," he said after I told him what had happened.

It wasn't long before his police car pulled up outside. He hurried in with another officer, his gaze going to where I stood hunched over my counter.

"Are you all right?"

Was that phrase to be our opening every time we met? "Just a little shaken," I answered. "As far as I can tell there's no sign of a break-in. So I don't know how they got in or what they were looking for."

"We'll take a look around, " Jerry said, patting me on the arm. I watched him conversing with the other officer who I didn't recognize, and then the two them went into the back of the store. I heard the squeak of the back door opening and closing and a few minutes later I heard footsteps in the apartment above the store. A minute later one of them knocked on the locked door at the bottom of the stairs leading up. As soon as I unlocked it Jerry swung the door open and came into the store. "Someone's been living up there," he announced.

"What?" All the horror from our first case together washed over me. My mother's evil twin and my father had been living in the second floor apartment for over a month before I'd realized it. After their deaths I'd put strong locks on the doors and cleared out all the furniture.

"Looks like it's some homeless person who managed to pick the outside lock."

The apartment had a separate entrance, which had worked well when the store was still a house. Since the incident with Vivienne and Frank I only kept boxes up there. "Why would a homeless person do this?" I gestured at the mess and then noticed several customers about to enter. I hurried toward the front door. "We're closed today," I said, trying to smile. "Inventory."

Mrs. Browning peered around me, her observant gaze taking in the disorder. "Looks like more than inventory, my dear," she said.

Thankfully she turned away and encouraged the others to do the same. I noticed that the rain had stopped for the moment, but clouds still rolled by, looking like they were running from something. I headed back to where Jerry and the other officer were examining the jumble of books, boxes, and papers and the broken glass.

"Is anything missing?" Jerry asked.

"I don't know. I haven't checked."

"See if you can determine that while we scout around a bit more. You'll need to redo the locks on the apartment, and if I were you I'd put in a security system."

I watched him head away, noticing for the first time that he'd shaved off his beard and cut his hair. He looked more like the Jerry I was familiar with as he went through his customary routine, nodding to the other cop as they examined the room. I wondered idly if being undercover had caused him to go a little crazy. If I'd been living with a bunch of drugged out loonies, I knew how crazy I would have been.

Jerry was upstairs when I went into the back and got

a broom and dustbin and began to clean up. I restacked the books on the shelves and then printed out an inventory sheet to see if anything was missing. As far as the essential oils were concerned, there was no way I could decipher the mess of glass on the floor. And now my newly purchased gift items were all broken as well.

By the time I'd cleaned up Jerry was back, his worried gaze on my face. "This is a lot coming on the heels of the other thing," he said quietly. "Do you have any idea who would do this?"

"Maybe that guy who came in the other day looking for a vapor machine? Is he one of the meth-head guys?"

"Was he a filthy dirt-bag with bad teeth?"

I laughed. "Pretty much. You know, now that that I think about it, I had a couple of letters from you and some pictures of us together in a folder in my desk. It's gone."

Jerry blanched. "Are you sure? If Cable did this he now knows exactly who I am."

"But you aren't doing that case anymore, are you? I mean, you shaved your beard and cut your hair."

Jerry nodded. "I told you the chief decided I needed therapy, said I was losing it."

I scoffed. "You told me she took you off the case but you didn't tell me why. You seem better than you did a couple of weeks ago."

Jerry stared at the floor looking embarrassed. "I stopped doing drugs. I'm in rehab."

It was then I noticed that his hands were shaking slightly. "What kind of drugs, Jerry?"

But at that moment the other officer appeared from upstairs. "I've dusted for prints up there—anything else, boss?"

Jerry shifted his attention from me. "Naw. Just call

the security people and get them out here, would you?" When the other officer pulled out his cell phone and punched in some numbers Jerry turned his attention back to me. "I don't want you to open the store again until you have a security system in place as well as changing those locks. Can you get that done in the next couple of days?"

I nodded and then watched the two of them head toward the front door. Jerry turned just before he left the store, his dark eyes finding mine. "Therapist says we have to talk," he said, and then he was gone.

Didn't he remember that we'd already talked and it had been a disaster? I shook my head and carried the sack of detritus out the back door and threw it in the garbage can. Maybe his therapist could see me too. I certainly felt like I needed her help after nearly being raped and now having my store ransacked.

At a little before three Agnes arrived at the store looking fragile and pale, dark circles in the hollows below her eyes. I hurried out the door so she wouldn't see the mess inside.

"Are you up to this? You look exhausted."

Agnes smiled wanly. "I'm fine. Just a hangover."

Agnes never overindulged so I knew this to be a lie, but I didn't say anything as I followed her out to her brand new Fiat 500.

I kept up a one-sided conversation about nothing as we drove to Once Again, wondering what in the world was going on with my friend. I was glad when we reached the store, feeling exhausted from trying to make conversation. If she didn't snap out of it soon I would have to confront her.

Five minutes after we entered Once Again Agnes found two dresses for me to try on—one was black lace and the other a mauve color with a low cut back. She handed them to me and then told me she was heading to the bathroom in back.

I tried on the black one first and found that it fit me perfectly. I liked the lacy look of the bodice and the square neckline that showed off my collarbones. It nipped in at the waist and hung gracefully to my ankles. It would go well with her dress. The mauve looked terrible on me. When she returned I was still preening in front of the mirror. "What do you think?" I asked.

She nodded. "I like it."

When she moved to the bench to sit down I took a long look at her, noticing that her skin looked almost green. "Agnes, what is going on with you?" I asked, pulling off the dress. "You don't seem well and I'm beginning to worry."

Agnes looked up at me, her dark eyes wide. "If you must know, I'm pregnant," she whispered.

I let out a little whoop. "That's great news! Why didn't you say?"

"I haven't told Sam and I'm afraid he'll be upset. I've been trying to decide whether to keep it or not."

I pulled on my jeans and shirt and sat next to her. "There's no way Sam will be anything but thrilled, Agnes. Why would you think otherwise?"

"He comes from a conservative family and if we have a baby a couple of months early everyone will know."

"The wedding is less than a month away and screw his family. This is about the two of you. Have you been to a doctor?"

"Not yet. And it's been really difficult to keep Sam from noticing the morning sickness. Last weekend it was so bad I had to pretend I had the flu."

"I knew you didn't have a hangover," I said, chuckling. "Is this why you've been so freaked out about the shooting?"

Agnes nodded, her hands coming over her face. "I kept imagining one of those kids belonging to me, to us."

I put my hand on her shoulder. "You have to tell him."

"But what if he doesn't want a baby? We haven't even discussed a family yet."

"He'll be thrilled, I'm sure of it. I've seen the way he looks at you—it's like you're a goddess."

Agnes giggled. "A fat goddess."

I grabbed her hand, pulling her up. "Come on. Let's pay for this and go celebrate. I'll have a glass of wine and you can have a ginger ale."

Agnes gave me a smirk. "Oh yeah, I forgot that part. Do you think one glass would hurt?"

"It's up to you, but all the evidence…"

Agnes raised her hand. "Okay, okay," she said.

She followed me up to the counter where I paid for my dress and then we walked to her sage green Fiat and headed to Saffron and Seaweed where we could have something yummy to accompany our beverages. Despite my bad memory of coming here with Jim, it was the best restaurant in town, and it was a good time to nail down details for the catering. It wasn't until after we had our drinks in hand that I told her about the break-in at Tarot and Tea. And after that I told her about the near rape and the coven meeting—in that order. At least it took her mind off her own troubles.

9

I met the security people and the locksmith at Tarot and Tea at eight o'clock sharp on Monday morning. By the time they'd left and I'd opened the store for business it was nearly lunchtime. Becky arrived at noon with a turkey sandwich for me.

"How did you know?" I asked, before taking a big bite.

She lifted her brows. "I'm a witch, didn't you know?"

I laughed. "I'd forgotten about your psychic powers."

"So how is the bride-to-be?"

I thought about Agnes's news, wondering if I should share it. The answer was no. "Nervous as a cat on a hot tin roof."

Becky laughed. "I like that imagery. I hope she doesn't quit the coven once she's married."

"Actually, she might. She told me Sam doesn't approve, but the man was intimately involved in Jerry's and my last case, so I'm not sure I believe her assessment. One of these days I'm going to have to ask him."

"So how is Ames's hottest detective?"

I knew she was talking about Jerry and held out my hands, palms up. "He's different every time I see him. According to his therapist we need to talk, so I'll probably see him again soon. He was a complete jerk the last time we got together, but then again he was very kind after the incident with Jim and about the break-in. He told me he's been in rehab."

"Jerry is a druggie?"

"He was embedded with a bunch of meth-heads in the woods west of town and god knows what he was doing."

Becky stared into space, a funny look on her face. "There's something out there…something that has to do with the shooting," she said dreamily. Her green eyes met mine. "Where was I?"

"You just told me that something was out there—where, though? In the woods?"

"I did? I must have had a vision, but it's gone now."

"Becky, maybe you need to come down to the station. They're arresting Sarah Cumberland for the murders, and I know she didn't do it."

Becky stared at me. "No, Sarah did not do it," she intoned.

"Do you know who did?"

Becky shook herself. "I have to go back to the store. I left Tim in charge, and if anyone comes in he's incapable of working the cash register. See you soon."

She was gone before I could answer, strawberry blonde braids flapping in the breeze as she hurried toward Daily Bread on the far corner. Her store was the only place on the street where the sun was shining, the rest of the area covered in threatening gray clouds.

After Becky left I had a steady influx of customers, all anxious to discuss the break-in. When I finally asked how they knew, they said they'd heard it from someone who heard it from someone who heard it from Mrs. Browning. I smiled inwardly, thinking about the gray-haired crone who had become a fixture in the store. I hoped my assessment that she was a ghost was correct— that way I would never have to lose her company.

It was nearing three o'clock when Jerry called me from his cell phone. "Are you free tonight?" he asked.

"I don't have any plans, if that's what you're asking."

"I can bring a bottle of wine or some food if that would help."

I let out a sigh. "I have some leftovers from the rack of lamb I made last night. If you want to come around seven we can have dinner together." As soon as I hung up I mentally chastised myself, reminding the part of me that still had feelings for the man that this Jerry was someone I did not know. He was as fickle as the wind and I couldn't predict how he would be this time. I would probably regret allowing him to come over. But then I remembered his rescue and how sweet he'd been with me after my near rape—he'd spent the entire night in the chair watching over me. I couldn't help but love him.

I was home waiting for him when my cell phone chimed—Jerry. I picked up on the second ring. "Where are you?"

"Sorry, Summer, I got waylaid by my mother. She made dinner and everything. I can't leave. Can I call you later?"

Jerry's mother and I did not get along, and this feeble excuse pissed me off. "Fine. I'll be here," I said. I hit end and threw my phone down, wondering why I felt on the verge of tears. All he wanted to do was clear the air about the break-up. Damn him and his bedroom eyes, his touch that always made me feel weak inside.

It was nearly ten when he finally called back. "I'm sorry it's so late. I'd come by but I've got to be at the police station early tomorrow."

"You wouldn't come by because I'm about to go to bed," I said huffily. "Do you want to tell me what this is all about?"

"I need to see you for this, Summer. Cynthia is convinced I'm—I mean she wants me to talk to you about our break-up. She thinks I've been avoiding you and the past. According to her I can't move forward until—"

"Until you've received my blessing? God, Jerry, you can be such a jerk."

"Summer, I—I'm sorry if I hurt you. I've been hurting to."

"Oh really? Is that why you stood me up tonight and went to your mother's instead?"

"Stood you up? I was just coming over to talk."

"We made a plan, I cooked. As far as I'm concerned you stood me up."

There was a long moment of silence. "I hadn't thought about it like that. I just figured you'd rather not see me and that this would be a way out for you."

"Don't assume you know what's going on with me. I was actually looking forward to hashing out the past. I've been caught up in it way too much."

"Can I have a rain check?"

I stared at the bedroom window covered in raindrops. "When?"

"This week is a bear. Let's do Friday evening. Will that work for you?"

"Around six?"

"Yeah, I can be there by then. Will you cook this time?"

I heard the hint of the old Jerry in his tone. He liked

my cooking and he and I had made a lot of meals together. "If you bring wine."

I hung up feeling slightly mollified, but I had to stop myself from sinking into fantasies about us getting back together. I was not going down that road again.

My dreams that night featured Jerry, the two of us as we had been before the last disastrous case. I got up early and took a run, trying to clear my head before leaving for Tarot and Tea. We are not getting back together, we are not getting back together, I said over and over like a mantra as my feet hit the damp pavement and my breath came out in little white gasps. By the time I got home I was drenched in sweat. I had to shower before I went to work or my customers would never venture in the door.

Jerry called me twice over the next few days—first to ask about the wedding and what he was required to wear in his capacity as best man—I referred him to Sam and Agnes—and also to ask about the shop and whether the security system was working.

"Everything is fine," I told him. "Thanks for calling them for me. They did a good job and didn't cost much."

"Can you have coffee with me in the morning?" he asked.

Tomorrow was Thursday, the day before he was coming over for dinner. "It can't wait until Friday?"

"This is something unrelated. I can pick you up early and drop you at Tarot and Tea. I have some news you might find interesting."

We settled on a time and hung up.

That night after I went to bed I couldn't get Jerry out of my mind. I thought about Jim Salazar again, my near rape looming large in my over-reactive mind. I wondered if the coffee tomorrow was about Jim.

I was waiting outside when Jerry arrived in the squad car. When I was walking toward the car I saw my neighbor peeking out from behind her curtain. I waved and she disappeared, the curtain falling back into place. I opened the door and slid in. "Neighbor is watching and wondering," I said, glancing at Jerry.

"Same neighbor who hates your dog?"

"The very same."

Jerry grinned. "Is Down and Dirty okay by you?"

Down and Dirty was a local coffee shop that made great lattes. "You're the expert on coffee, Jerry. I bow to your choice."

Once we were seated and had ordered coffee Jerry gazed at me. By the look on his face I knew what he had to say would be upsetting.

"Sarah has been indicted. And I talked with Myra Proctor, the DA. Jim Salazar has been blacklisted. He won't be getting any more business from her office, or anyone else's, I would imagine. I charged him with attempted rape but you know how that goes—he's out on bail. At least he'll lose his PI's license. I wish I could throw the book at him."

"Does that mean I'll have to testify?"

"Probably, but it's months down the road."

"Do you think he's dangerous?"

"No, but I'd keep your eyes open. Any guy who runs around drugging women has got to be somewhat off."

I stared out the window thinking about martial arts. Unfortunately being a black belt in something wouldn't have helped. "Thanks, Jerry."

"You don't have to thank me—thank Myra and the fact that she's an honest woman who's interested in justice. This could have gone very differently if that had not been the case."

"I was wondering if it was Jim who broke into Tarot and Tea—it seemed just like a petty thing he would do."

"But why would he take a folder of pictures of you and me, and letters I wrote to you?"

"Yeah—I think you're right—it had to be Cable."

Just before we left the coffee shop two men came in wearing camouflage-hunting jackets. They gave us hostile looks before settling into a small table in the back corner. I strained to hear their conversation but the only words I could make out were 'we'll be ready when the time comes'. Ready for what? We left the coffee shop a few minutes later and climbed back in the squad car. When Jerry pulled up in front of my store he left the car idling. "See you tomorrow night?" I said, getting out of the car.

He gave a nod and watched me head inside before rolling away.

On Friday my store was as busy as I'd seen it in a long time. An older man maybe in his late sixties bought several crystal paperweights and asked me all about the shooting. "I lived here a long time ago," he told me. "I was good friends with the Cumberland family. I was shocked when I heard that Sarah was a suspect."

"How did you hear?"

His eyes slid sideways. "I must have read it in the paper. I wish I could do something to help her."

I was pretty sure this bit of news hadn't been in the paper, but I didn't argue, just handed him his paperweights wrapped in bubble-wrap. "Thanks for coming in."

Several couples came in after he left and I heard them whispering together in the stacks. I pretended to be straightening shelves as I tried to catch their conversation. "It's the work of the devil," one woman whispered, picking up a crystal and a talisman in the shape of a goddess. She placed them back and visibly shuddered. "Let's get out of here."

I moved back to the counter feeling sick inside. They were in my store because they thought I was a devil worshiper. The town was on the verge of hysteria, ready to take matters into its own hands. I wasn't surprised when they hurried out without buying anything.

Just as I was closing up Becky stopped by, a newspaper in her hands. "Have you seen this?" She held it out.

TOWN OF AMES POISED ON THE BRINK OF MADNESS DUE TO GRIEF.

A group of Ames men has been combing the woods to find the possible perpetrator of the school shooting two weeks ago. A well-known pastor at the local church has been preaching fire and brimstone, fanning the flames of their anger and loss. He is preaching the gospel according to Matthew 5:38, an eye for an eye. The mood has rapidly escalated from grief to fury, and even with the arrest of one of our own citizens, Sarah Cumberland, there is still a troubling mood that has not diminished. There has been talk of the 'devil's work', as though Sarah

Cumberland is part of a cult that needs to be ferreted out. Are we living in the 1600's where the citizens can claim witchcraft and go after anyone they deem a witch? Or will sense prevail? This reporter hopes it is the latter.

I looked up. "This is completely nuts."

Becky nodded. "I've overheard several conversations this past week about cults. If we're not careful we could be targeted."

"You mean the coven?"

"That's exactly what I mean. This dark mood is escalating, Summer. I say we curtail our meetings until this blows over."

"And now they've arrested Sarah who didn't do it. We need to help her."

"The only way to help Sarah is to find the real murderer. Without hard evidence the townspeople will still be screaming for blood."

10

When I left the store the sky had turned an inky shade of gray, wind whipping around the sides of houses as though picking up the mood of the town. My scarf blew off and when I tried to catch it I tripped on a downed branch and went flying to my knees. A second later a man hurried by me without stopping, his furtive gaze suspicious. I pushed myself up and continued on.

Once I was across from the market I noticed small groups of men huddled together talking. Some of them were armed. Was open carry even allowed here? Pauline was standing in the doorway, a worried look on her face, and when I waved she didn't wave back. When the first drop of rain hit my bare head I began to jog, making it home just before the sky opened up.

I fed Mischief and Cutty, listening to the wind whine around my house like some malevolent force attempting to get inside. Lightning lit up the sky followed quickly by the boom of thunder, tree limbs banging on my roof and windows, detritus flying all over the place. I saw my lidless garbage can fly by at nearly window height, trash spewing from it like confetti, spreading from one end of the alley to the other. Luckily the main house in back was vacant at the moment, the wealthy family that owned it away on one of their world tours, or some such thing. If they had been there I would have heard non-stop complaints about my slovenly ways.

Just before seven my door blew open, banging on the wall behind it. Jerry appeared wearing his motorcycle helmet and leather jacket, both wet. He pushed the door closed and locked it. "Jesus, what a storm," he said, pulling off his helmet. "I almost lost control of the bike on the way over here."

"I can't believe you drove the bike, Jerry. Don't you have a handy police car stashed at your house?"

He scoffed and removed his jacket and hung it on my wooden coat rack. "I guess I like a good challenge."

"Dangerous and foolhardy, you mean?"

"Hey, hey, let's be nice here. I promised to be good and you have to promise too."

"I don't remember you making that promise."

He was so much like the old Jerry that I had to stop myself from rushing into his arms. He even looked the same, with his tousled brown hair, his cheeks ruddy from the wind and cold. He was wearing worn jeans and a gray linen shirt that fit him well. I watched him roll up the sleeves exposing the small tattoo of a Celtic knot on his right forearm, an homage to his Irish heritage on his father's side he'd had done after his father's death.

"I brought a bottle of wine," he announced, pulling one from his jacket pocket.

"Can't believe that survived," I said, taking the Merlot. I looked at the label, noticing the one we both had favored when we were together. I took it into the kitchen and retrieved the corkscrew, watching Jerry out of the corner of my eye. He was looking around my living room as though he'd never been there before.

A second later Cutty flew out of the bedroom and rushed toward him. Before I could stop him Cutty had launched himself into Jerry's arms. "Hey, little guy,"

Jerry crooned, cuddling my dog. "At least you still like me." He caught my eye and I had to look away to hide my smile.

"Everything's ready," I called a few minutes later, setting the dishes on the table. I poured wine into two glasses and placed them on the table. A second later the lights flickered and went out. "Oh great," I muttered, searching through the drawer where I kept the candles. Jerry found a couple of tapers in one of my other hiding places and lit them from my gas stove, placing them in the antique silver candle holders that always sat on my table. The light was soft and more romantic than I had envisioned for this visit.

"Did you use your old key to get in or did I leave the door open?" I asked, handing him a dish of new potatoes and trying to let go of my nerves.

"I still have the key. You should have changed the locks."

"I didn't need to since you never came by."

We ate mostly in silence, except for the compliments Jerry gave me regarding the food. When we were finished I loaded everything into the dishwasher I'd recently had installed, and Jerry and I cleaned up the remaining dishes, covering the leftovers and placing them in the refrigerator. "I guess I'll have to wait until tomorrow to turn it on."

"You never know," Jerry said, carrying another candle into the living room and inserting it into a holder he found in one of the cabinets.

"I think what I miss most about you not living here is your espresso machine," I said, following him in.

"Well, that makes me feel great."

But I knew by his tone that he wasn't irritated by my comment. "Want your wine?"

"Please. And if you have another candle it's kind of dark in here."

I grabbed one off the table and managed to carry it, two glasses, and the wine bottle with me. I refilled his glass and settled on the loveseat, watching shadows flicker across his clean-shaven cheek. A minute went by and then another as we sipped our wine, listening to the unearthly howl of the wind.

Finally Jerry said, "Cynthia wants me to get clear with you. She says I've bottled up a lot of feelings and that's why I got into drugs."

I put my glass down on the table. "That makes sense to me. Is she the same therapist you had before?"

"The one you said was a shitty therapist? Yup, same one. And by the way, I told her what you said."

I peered at him but couldn't make out his expression. "What was her response?"

"She laughed and said she would probably like you." Jerry placed his glass on the table and leaned forward. "Summer, what I did to you was unforgiveable. I'm sorry for all of it."

"What are these bottled up feelings you have?"

Jerry looked away, and a second later a tree limb banged against the side of the house making us both jump. "Should I go and check?" he asked.

I shook my head. "It's too crazy out there to do anything about it. I'll discover all the damage tomorrow." I watched him collect himself, his fingers running through his thick hair. He took another sip of wine before he continued.

Liquid courage, I thought to myself, picking up my own glass.

"Cynthia thinks I'm still in love with you," he suddenly said.

I was so shocked I couldn't speak for a moment, finally squeaking out, "Sam said you were dating another woman."

"What? No. No other woman. I was probably hoping to get back with you when I said that, and then all hell broke loose."

"By hell breaking loose do you mean the shooting?"

"Yeah, partly, and the case with these junkies, Jim Salazar, and the break-in at your store."

"When Cynthia suggested you might still be in love with me, what did you say?"

When he looked up it seemed to me that his eyes were more liquid than before. "I told her that I miss us. It's why I took that undercover job—it was just dangerous enough to keep me from thinking about you."

I looked away, feeling my face grow hot. I hadn't expected to have this conversation.

"Cynthia asked me to explore my feelings regarding you—us—and to talk with you about your feelings. How do you feel about me, Summer—aside from being pissed off?"

"I still love you, Jerry," I said before I could stop myself. "But—"

"But I'm an asinine prick and you want nothing to do with me?"

I had to laugh at that. "Not exactly. It's more of a trust issue. And what happened with Jim didn't help. I've seen several sides of you these past weeks, and I'm not sure who the real Jerry is. Tonight you seem like your old self but who will you be tomorrow?"

Jerry nodded and put his face in his hands. "I can't tell you how upset I was when I came in here and found that bastard about to—" He shook his head. "That guy should be horse-whipped." Jerry picked up his wine again and took a long swallow. "Now that I'm off the drugs I can think more clearly, and what's been coming up for me over and over is what I feel for you." He looked up. "I love you, Summer. I never stopped. It's just that my ego and all the rest of it got in the way."

I felt a little shock in my heart region. "Are you dealing with this in therapy?"

"Of course I am."

"What about the ghosts, my 'weirdness' as you called it?"

"Ego—it's all about my ego. I had no idea how insecure I was until you solved that damn case."

"I didn't know how insecure I was until you and your old girlfriend, Maria, started hanging out together."

Jerry laughed. "I was way over Maria a long time ago. Maybe we shouldn't talk about all that—focus more on the present. Are you dating anyone?"

"No, Jerry, I'm not, but that doesn't mean—"

"I know, I know. I look at you now and it seems like we never split up."

"Where have you been living, on another planet? I've had to deal with this for nearly ten months. And believe me, I felt every moment of it."

"Sam told me you were with another guy. What happened to him?"

I shook my head. "He wanted to move in and when I said no he split."

"So no real break-up, then. What's to keep him from showing up one of these days and expecting you to be here waiting for him?"

"I guess he could, but if he did I'd tell him to get lost. Tom acted like an over protective mother and it drove me crazy."

"And this Jim—you went out with him. What would

have happened if he'd been a normal guy?"

"Why are you asking all these questions? Jim is not a normal guy and even if he was I wouldn't have fallen into bed with him, if that's what you want to know."

Jerry rose from the chair and moved to the loveseat next to me. "I'm sorry," he said, taking hold of my hand. "If I could do it over, I would."

Our eyes met and then he leaned forward and kissed me. It seemed like an innocent enough kiss when it began—a make-up kiss, nothing more than that. I would like to say I pulled away, but I didn't. Instead my arms went round him and our lips clung together in a sort of searching poignant moment that lasted quite a long time. When we pulled apart he searched my face. "Are you okay with this? I mean after what happened and—"

"I love you," I answered. And that was what broke the dam.

I woke in the morning in Jerry's arms with Cutty pressed against my back. When I tried to extricate myself he pulled me close again. "Don't go away," he murmured in my ear.

"But don't you—"

"Don't talk," he said, kissing my neck. And that was the last thing I remembered for a while, the feel of him against me as natural as breathing.

Much later I made coffee in my crappy machine, almost embarrassed to give him a cup. I was late for work, he was late for work, and neither one of us seemed to care. The storm had raged all night, keeping time with our heightened senses and labored breathing. The electricity was still out and the streets looked as though a hurricane had passed through, my body feeling the same way. We ate some cold cereal before he headed for the door. "When can I move back in?" he asked me, grinning.

I frowned and shook my head. "I think we should take this slow," I answered.

"Is that what we did last night—take it slow?"

I tried to look serious but I ended up breaking out in laughter. "Talk to Cynthia and see what she says," I finally said. "I'll go along with any advice she gives you."

But when he had closed the door I mentally reprimanded myself. Jerry was coming off a long undercover job and had been recently hooked on drugs. He was in no condition to make a commitment to me and I was foolish to think he could.

11

After Jerry left for the police station I cleaned up the yard and dragged all the downed limbs into a pile at the side of the house. So far I couldn't see any damage to my roof, but I hadn't crawled up there to inspect it closely. There were a few shingles on the ground and I hoped I wouldn't have leaks as a result. Maybe Jerry could take a look, I thought, and then chastised myself—one night of fabulous sex didn't mean we were back together.

When Agnes called I was walking along a street filled with every manner of trash, heading toward Tarot and Tea.

"Did you tell Sam?" I asked as soon as we greeted one another.

There was a pause. "I think I'm going to postpone the wedding," Agnes said.

"What are you talking about? Everything's set up and paid for—why would you do that?"

"I feel sick all the time and I'm afraid my bump will show."

"Agnes, you are bone thin. You probably won't show until you're six months along. And if you postpone you'll only be bigger!"

"I'm afraid, Summer. I'm afraid I'll be a bad mother and that something terrible will happen to the baby." She began to cry. "I'm going to have an abortion."

"Agnes, please tell Sam before you make a decision like this—he's the father—he has a right to know."

"If I do it now he'll never know."

"And it will be something huge between you—believe me, you'll never get over it. I'm not against you getting an abortion, I'm just saying you should make this decision together."

"Can you come over?"

"Let me check on my store and let everyone know it's closed for the day, and then I'll get a taxi, unless you want to come pick me up?"

"I'll be at Tarot and Tea at noon."

To my relief, the store seemed to have come through the storm unscathed. I had a couple of small leaks back in the kitchen area, but other than that all was well, including my kitty, who seemed unperturbed about it all. Once I saw the Fiat drive up I put my closed sign in the door, gave my cat another rub and headed out. No point in setting the alarm since there was no electricity here either. Apparently the entire town was down.

Agnes looked like she hadn't slept, her dark eyes huge in her pale face. "You look terrible," I said, regretting the words the second they were out of my mouth.

"Thanks a lot—that's just what a bride wants to hear. That's another reason to postpone."

"Usually the morning sickness goes away. How many months are you?"

"I think about three. It's almost too late to do anything about it."

"Agnes, if you don't tell Sam I will. I'm not kidding about this."

"You wouldn't!"

"Yes, I would. I love and respect you, but this is over the top, and I think your lack of sleep has addled your brain."

Agnes didn't answer as she maneuvered the car around trashcans, bags of trash, downed limbs and wooden shingles. "What a crazy storm," she muttered.

In the living room she'd set up several old oil lamps that gave off a soft light. She lit a few candles she'd placed strategically and then flopped onto the soft leather couch and let out a long sigh. "God, I don't know what to do."

"Listen to your best friend and do the right thing. If you haven't told him by tonight I'm telling Jerry, and Jerry will tell him."

Agnes swiveled to look at me. "Jerry?"

Blood came into my cheeks, giving me away.

Agnes sat up and stared at me. "You're back together."

"Not exactly."

Agnes grinned. "You had sex."

I smiled and nodded. "We're going to take it slow."

"Good luck with that."

The door opened a second later and Sam came in. "What's happening here?" he asked coming over to Agnes and kissing the top of her head. "Feel any better, sweet one?"

"A little," she smiled. "Did you know Summer and Jerry are—?"

Sam grinned and looked at me. "Jerry told me. I'm really glad to hear it." Sam stared into the distance for a moment his expression darkening. "As long as you're here I may as well tell you that Sarah Cumberland has asked for counsel. I argued with the chief about her arrest because I 'm sure she didn't have anything to do with it, but unfortunately we have no other suspects and the town is out for blood."

"What about that guy, Cable? Jerry thinks he may have had something to do with it."

"We don't have any evidence on him."

"Can't you bring him and grill him?"

Sam laughed, a hollow sound. "You've seen too many cop shows. He could be the shooter, but without solid evidence we're kind of SOL."

"Why don't you raid the meth lab and bring him in for questioning?"

"We could do that, but we already have the murder weapon. If Sarah didn't do this, someone went to a lot of trouble to pin it on her."

When Sam left to change into his sweats I glanced at Agnes. "Now is the perfect time to tell him," I said. "Go in there and do it."

"With you out here?"

"Why not? You can come out together and share the momentous news with me."

"What if he freaks out?"

I grabbed her by the hand and pulled her up. "Go."

While she was gone I sent a text message to Jerry. *At Agnes's house. Are you coming by tonight?*

Can I? I've been thinking about you all day.

Yes, and me too. Maybe you could pick me up?

Ah ha, hidden agenda. I'll see you in a couple of hours.

It was a good forty minutes before Agnes and Sam reappeared. Agnes looked more relaxed than I'd seen her in recent weeks and Sam was beaming. "We're going to have a baby!" he announced, heading into the kitchen. "I'm opening some bubbly to celebrate. I am seriously the luckiest man alive."

I glanced at Agnes who met my gaze. "That is wonderful news," I said, raising my eyebrows in an expression of 'I told you so.' "When is the baby due?" I asked innocently.

"Sometime in November? I guess I should go see a doctor."

"I know a good one," Sam said, coming back holding three full glasses of champagne. He handed them around. "She's a friend of my sister's and does a lot of natural birthing. Are you into that, Ags?"

"I don't know since I've never been pregnant before."

"She is," I said before taking a sip. "Any self-respecting witch will go for the natural way."

Agnes gave me a sharp look but Sam didn't even blink an eye. "This is the best news," he said, sitting next to Agnes and looping an arm around her shoulders. "It explains why you've been so pale and sickly. I was really worried, babe."

"I'm sorry Sam. I should you have told you sooner, but I didn't know how you'd take it."

"You didn't know—are you kidding?" He reached over and kissed her.

I gave her a look and she smirked back at me.

By the time Jerry arrived, the three of us had nearly gone through another bottle of champagne. I noticed that it was mostly Sam and me who were drinking, but Agnes did have a little of it, whispering that the bubbly couldn't be bad for the baby.

Sam told Jerry the news the minute he walked through the door. Jerry glanced at me in a meaningful way before congratulating Sam and taking the glass Sam held out.

He took a sip and sat next to me. "I hate to be the bearer of bad news, especially at a time like this, but the noose is tightening around Sarah. We have to find some evidence to prove her innocence before the chief officially closes the case."

"I told Sam about Cable, Jerry. If he doesn't have something to do with it, I bet he knows who did."

"I agree, but proving it is a different story. What do you say, Sam—set up a raid? I'd like to get rid of those bastards once and for all, even if one of them isn't the shooter."

Sam frowned. "The chief has been funny about them for some reason. It's like she knows one of them personally or something."

Jerry stared at his partner. "I've had the same thought. She's never even hinted that we should bring their enterprise down even after all my time embedded with them. Can we do this on our own?"

"Only if we make up some story for why we had to do it."

"They made me—that's a good enough reason. We had to do it before they scattered like rats in a flood."

"We'll need back-up," Sam said, standing and beginning to pace. "Let's get Simon and Al to come with us. They'll go for the secrecy if we explain what we're doing."

Jerry nodded. "We'll have to go in with guns blazing in the middle of the night. Those dudes are armed to the teeth."

I blanched as I imagining Jerry being gunned down. "Is four men enough?"

Sam turned my way. "Should be if they don't expect us."

By the time Jerry and I left for my house the plan had been solidified, even down to calling Al and Simon. It would happen the next night at two o'clock in the morning. A sensation of dread lodged itself under my breastbone.

Cutty was very happy to see us when we walked into the dark house. I flipped the light switch, surprised when the overhead light turned on. "Electricity is back."

"Crap. I was looking forward to a bath and candles," Jerry murmured, looking at me with one eyebrow cocked.

"Yes, but without electricity the water wouldn't have been hot."

"Oh yeah, I forgot about that." Jerry turned away, his gaze going toward the kitchen. "I'm hungry," he said heading in like he owned it. I watched him open the refrigerator and take out the leftovers from the night before.

I came into the kitchen behind him, got the silverware out of the drawer and set the table. At this moment it felt like the ten months we'd been apart had never happened. But I knew better.

12

The bed beside me was empty when I woke in the morning. Not surprising considering the argument we'd had when I questioned his plan. He didn't like being asked how many meth-heads there would be or what kind of weapons they might have on hand. Our heated discussion had continued late into the night, steering into more personal areas that we hadn't touched since we'd broken up. At one in the morning Jerry had finally had enough, announcing that until they'd taken custody of the suspects he'd prefer to stay at his house. Of course I was tearful and apologetic, but in the end he'd jumped on his motorcycle and roared away.

At least we'd managed to hash out some of the problems still lingering from our last case, including his attitude about my ghosts. He said he still had a few doubts, but since the chief seemed to believe in me, he was less inclined to dismiss it as utter nonsense.

"Thanks a lot! You always said you believed me," I had told him petulantly, which led to another round of shouting.

I sighed and rose from the tangled sheets and pulled the blanket I'd thrown off in the middle of night, back on the bed. I tucked it in, straightened the bedclothes and went to get a cup of coffee. Somehow while I was at work the day before Jerry had brought over his espresso machine, and its presence in my kitchen calmed me. It seemed a symbol of commitment. Wouldn't he have taken it with him if he'd decided not to come back? Although on second thought how could he have carried it with him on his motorcycle?

Why in the world was I allowing this thing to go ahead when I knew Jerry was still dealing with his drug addiction? I knew from experience that we needed to have a good long talk about what we were doing. He hadn't mentioned anything about his therapist and what she might have said about this new development. And besides, hadn't I mentioned taking it slow? I shook my head, spooning ground coffee into the little basket. Maybe we were just shacking up for a while. That thought did nothing for my mood. Clearly I'd already been swept into the Jerry Brady charm.

When I reached Tarot and Tea customers were waiting, including my best ghost customers, Douglas and Mrs. Browning. I'd lingered longer than I'd intended, drinking my espresso and daydreaming about past mornings with Jerry. I had to get a grip.

"The storm is past, Summer. Why are you late this morning?" Mrs. Browning asked grumpily.

"Sorry. I got caught up with—"

"Your new/old boyfriend?" she asked, staring at me pointedly.

How did she know that? "Well, no, not exactly. We aren't living together."

Mrs. Browning cocked her head and looked up at me, reminding me of a bird. "He should be careful," she said enigmatically. "The town is in a dangerous mood."

"Careful about what exactly?" I asked, but before she could answer my cat rushed out of the open door and disappeared under a particularly spiny rose bush. I hurried after her and managed to drag her out. "What got into you, Tabby?" I whispered, carrying her back inside and closing the door.

My customers had turned on the lights and scattered into the shelves, leaving me to investigate my cat's uncharacteristic behavior. I found out when I saw the door to the upstairs standing open. Was the homeless person up there, or someone more dangerous? I had my cell phone out and was about to call Jerry when Douglas came up behind me. "There's someone upstairs who wants to talk to you," he whispered.

"Who?"

"An old friend of mine who I haven't seen in sixty years."

"Sadie Cumberland," I whispered.

Douglas smiled and headed away to look at what was left of my essential oils.

I hurried into the closed stairwell, wondering what Sadie had to tell me this time. She was probably distraught about her granddaughter but there was nothing I could do about it until Jerry and Sam brought in that gang of thugs. And with the town in an uproar we had bigger things to worry about.

She was standing in what had been the living room, but now was filled with boxes, and for a second she seemed so alive that I thought she was Sarah, but a moment later she turned wispy and indistinct. "You must help my sweet girl," she whispered.

"To help her we have to find the real killer. Do you have any idea who it is?"

Sadie looked around the room, as though expecting eavesdroppers, and then leaned toward me. "Look at the weapon again," she said, and then she was gone.

What was it with these ghosts? Was there a rule saying they weren't allowed to help the living? I ran down the stairs and called the police station on my landline, listening to the options and the music impatiently—guess I should have called 911. When someone finally answered I asked to talk to the chief.

"Who's calling, please?" the female voice asked.

"This is Summer McCloud and I have information regarding the recent school shooting."

I waited for what seemed like eternity, listening to canned music and announcements about what the police did for the town, glad when I finally heard Sandra Marshall's voice.

"What can I do for you, Summer?"

"I think you should take another look at the murder weapon."

"And what would I be looking for?"

"Maybe prints, maybe something else, I don't know."

"Dare I ask where this came from?"

"Do you really want to know?"

There was a moment of silence. "No, I suppose not. It's a good thing I'm open-minded."

"Jerry and Sam don't think Sarah did it," I continued. "They—" I stopped myself before I gave away their plan.

"They what? Please tell me if Sam and Jerry are up to something. They've both been a thorn in my side ever since we took Sarah into custody."

"No. They just want to find the real murderer, that's all."

"All the evidence we have so far points in a straight line to Miss Cumberland. Until we have a reason to suspect someone else, she is all we have. Have you seen the groups of people hanging around outside the police station, Summer? They want closure and Sarah represents that. Thanks for calling. I'll have my team take another look at the weapon, but I don't expect to find anything new."

As soon as I hung up I called Jerry. "Are we on the outs again?" I asked.

"The outs? I told you I'd be staying away until after we arrest these bums. As soon as this caper is over I'll be in touch."

"Caper? That's what you're calling it? That sounds more like jewel thieves breaking into an empty mansion."

Jerry laughed. "What are you saying, Miss McCloud—are you worried about me?"

"I don't really like the idea of you lying in a pool of blood a second after we've made up."

Jerry scoffed. "I'd call what happened between us more like unbridled lust."

"Jerry, this isn't funny. Please be careful."

"I always am. Don't worry. I'll call you in the morning."

I hung up feeling a tiny bit better about us, but not relieved about what he and Sam were about to do. And I had the feeling that when the chief found out, she was not going to be happy about it, either.

By the time I'd closed up the shop and was heading home the wind had come up again, sending any remaining trash from the storm flying in all directions. I huddled into my jacket, hurrying down the street and trying not to think about the upcoming 'caper'. If something happened to Jerry—I shook myself and put my mind on the scene unfolding around me. For the first time I noticed the glow from television sets in every house I passed. Something had happened. I jogged the rest of the way, bursting into my house and scaring Cutty who had been asleep on the loveseat. "Sorry, Bud," I said, reaching down to scratch his ears. I hung up my jacket and headed to my computer.

Vigilantes discover meth lab in the woods west of Ames, was the first local news headline I discovered. I read through the article, finding out that the place was now deserted, any remnants of the guys Jerry had been planning to arrest, long gone—so much for getting Sarah off the hook. Why were the police allowing these crazy yahoos to comb through the woods and scare away anyone who might be the real killer?

My only hope now was that the weapon would reveal something—but what? The police must have taken all the fingerprints off it already. Was there another set they hadn't identified? I breathed a long sigh of relief as I realized that Jerry would not be out there in the wee hours. A second later my phone rang.

"Did you tell the chief about our plans?" Jerry demanded.

"No, Jerry. I only asked her to look at the weapon again—Sadie appeared to me and—"

"Sadie? Who is Sadie?"

"I thought I told you. Sadie Cumberland is Sarah's deceased grandmother."

"Oh yeah, you did. And her name came up in our investigation. You get your wish—I won't be lying in a pool of blood tonight after all."

"Don't joke about this. Who discovered the meth lab?"

"The chief sent her team out to see if they were still there. That's why I thought you'd said something."

"Was that before or after these crazies found it? The local news online said they're combing the woods, I guess looking for the cult that Sarah belongs to? Why don't you arrest them?"

"The police don't have the authority to arrest forty men for looking for the killer. But if those nutjobs shoot someone in the process then all bets are off."

"Are you coming over after work?"

"It depends."

"On what?"

"On whether Sam and I can track these jerks. I haven't given up on bringing them in."

"So the pool of blood is still possible," I muttered.

"The four of us are heading out now."

"Frankly I hope you don't find anything."

"Don't you want to get your friend off?"

"Not if it means losing you."

Jerry didn't say anything but I knew I'd struck a chord. We said goodbye after he promised, again, to be careful.

I stared out the window, seeing only my worried face reflected back. Sadie obviously knew a lot more than she was saying. And then I remembered Becky and her faraway look when she said *there's something out there.* She could have been referring to the guys and the meth lab, but I didn't think so. This case was becoming more and more disturbing. And with the townspeople taking the law into their own hands, it was only going to get worse.

I was sound asleep when Cutty began a wild barking. I sat up in bed, expecting Sadie again, but instead of a ghost a dark figure stood in my bedroom door. I was just about to scream when Jerry said, "It's only me."

I switched on my bedside lamp and watched him remove his gun and put it down on the bedside table.

"What happened?"

Jerry shook his head, his eyes on the belt he was unbuckling. "They're gone, along with any evidence. I think those crazy jerks from town were up there, because the place was literally torn apart. I swear the chief is involved in this in some way."

"Do you think she warned them or do you mean the men prowling the woods warned them?"

Jerry shook his head. "I suspect the chief before I suspect these vigilantes carrying guns. They don't know what the hell they're doing." Jerry unbuttoned his shirt and removed it, and then slipped off his jeans before crawling under the covers. He reached for me and I moved into his arms. "This case is getting to me," he said, nuzzling my neck.

I shifted my body and pulled him down next to me. "I know how to make you forget all about it," I murmured.

"Show me, Summer McCloud. I'm putty in your hands," Jerry whispered, his deft fingers moving along my back and sending shivers up and down my spine.

I maneuvered so that I could kiss him and then the two of us went someplace else for a quite a long while.

13

I was checking out a customer a few days later when my cell phone rang, startling me. I normally turned it off when I was busy, figuring if anyone had to get hold of me they could call the store number. "Agnes, what's up?"

"Sam told me what happened in the woods. Do you think one of those meth dealers is the murderer?"

"I don't know, but we have to find another suspect soon or Sarah is sunk."

"Sam says he's trying, but without having them in custody he's not sure how to manage it. He also told me that a group of angry parents are camped outside the police station. What has happened to this town?"

I gazed at a red-eyed woman browsing through my shelves. She glanced at me and picked up a book on Wiccan, a look of horror appearing on her face. I'd noticed several strangers the last few days, only here to make judgments about my store and me. "It's gone insane, that's what."

"What does Jerry say?" Agnes asked.

I thought about how we'd been making up for our time apart. "We haven't been talking about it."

Agnes laughed. "You mean you haven't been doing much talking, is that it?"

"Well..."

"I don't blame you. You need to get reacquainted.

Are you guys living together?"

"I don't know what we're doing. I told him I'd go along with what his therapist said, but I don't think he's seen her lately."

"I'm glad you'll be together for my wedding. It makes it a lot more special for Sam and me."

"How are you feeling? Did you go to the doctor?"

"Yes, and she's great. She told me to keep crackers with me for the morning sickness—she said it's because the baby needs glucose. Will you be my coach when the time comes?"

"Of course I will." I looked up as Douglas walked toward me. "Got to go, your father wants to buy something."

"Tell him hello. I haven't told him my news yet, so don't let it slip, okay?"

"I won't." I hung up and turned to Douglas. "And what can I do for you, sir?" I asked, smiling.

"Was that Agnes on the phone?"

"Yes. She said to say hello."

Douglas looked perplexed as he ran a hand through his silver gray hair. "I haven't seen her for several weeks and the last time I did, she seemed unwell. Is it still about the shooting?"

"You need to ask her," I answered, taking the small wooden box embedded with semi-precious stones he handed me. I rang him up, trying not to meet his perceptive gaze.

"She's going to have a baby," he said, as I handed him his change. "Which means I will be a grandpa."

I laughed. "How do you know that?"

"It's written all over you, and besides, I have a certain ability when it comes to thoughts."

"You're a mind reader?"

"Of sorts."

"Oh brother. Now I have to watch what I think."

Douglas chortled. "Your thoughts are sweet as can be, Summer. No worries there."

As soon as he said that I had a vision of Jerry and me lying naked on my bed. I could feel heat rise into my cheeks, but Douglas only smiled and walked toward the door. Despite being a ghost he'd been around the block a couple of times himself, and I knew he was, or had been, a very passionate man. He was still handsome—for all I knew he was shacked up with a woman right now.

My thoughts went to Mrs. Browning and her coven meetings, the goddess books she read, and all the people in town she knew. These local ghosts were conducting their lives like regular people who hadn't yet left this earth, and with a more enlightened attitude. You wouldn't see them rushing around searching for a cult that needed to be brought to justice.

When my cell phone rang a few minutes later I was still staring toward the door where I'd last seen Douglas, thinking about what he might be up to. Lately he had a look in his eye that I'd seen in the past—one that told me he was hiding something. The call was from the police station and I moved my finger across the screen to answer.

"Summer? Can you come down to the station?" The chief sounded distracted and somewhat frantic.

"I'm at work now. Can it be later on this afternoon?

Sandra Marshall let out a sigh. "Yes, but make it as soon as you can."

At four o'clock I began to close up the store, my mind on what the chief had to say. Since it was police business I used the excuse to call and ask Jerry for a ride.

"When are you going to get a car?" he asked in an irritated tone.

"I haven't had time to look. If it's that inconvenient I can call a taxi."

"I'd come, but I'm with Sam. We're scouting again, trying to get a bead on where those guys went."

"I'll call a taxi. See you tonight?"

"Hope so," he said, and then the line went dead.

Where in hell were they? And did the chief know what they were up to? I called the one small taxi company in town and locked up the shop. I waited by the curb watching the sky darken with clouds, hoping we wouldn't have another storm. It was cold for the end of May, and I hoped the day of Agnes's wedding would be better weather since we'd planned to have the reception on the porch and garden at the home.

The grounds had once been a beautiful place and Agnes had paid landscapers to bring it back to its former splendor. Now it was full of azalea bushes and rhododendron, roses interspersed between them. What had been dirt paths were graveled, and meandered through the mature cherry trees and the flowering shrubs, leading to a wide area in which an old stone fountain had been resurrected. Now water flowed from the mouth of the dragon that coiled at its edge, making a soft sound and attracting birdlife.

The taxi dropped me off at the station and I hurried inside out of the cold wind that was blowing for the third day in a row. I was moving toward the desk when I saw Sandra motioning me into her office.

"Please sit," she said, a frown of worry on her face. "We checked that gun again and found another set of prints we'd missed before. They are not in the system and I'm still trying to find out who they belong to."

"That's good for Sarah, right?"

"That's why I called you in. It's going to be hell to figure out who else held that weapon. It's been around for over seventy years. We've just begun to look in the database. But the good news is there was evidence of a break-in at Sarah's house. Whoever it was came in through the basement. Not sure how we missed it. We're gathering as much as we can from the window and hoping to match up the prints."

"How did they know the gun was there?"

"That's the question. I know you'd like to see Sarah freed, but until we find another suspect she's all we've got. As far as knowing about the gun, we've looked into her relatives who would have known about that weapon, but her mother is deceased and it appears there are no others. The main problem is that she's on suicide watch now."

"What? Why?"

"She's gone into a depression. I want you to talk to her."

"I hardly know her!"

"But you've met her grandmother and you feel that Sarah is innocent—that alone should help calm her down."

"I don't know if she believes in ghosts—I can't just blurt out that I've had visitations. Does she have a good lawyer?"

"He's court appointed since Sarah has little money. According to her he's not encouraging about her case." Sandra began to pace, her long fingers curling into fists. "The last thing I need right now is a suicide on my hands. The press is already all over us. Can I take you down to see her?"

"I guess so, but I don't know if I'll be much help."

"Just try, okay?"

When I saw Sarah I tried hard not to cry. The older woman had lost weight, her eyes hollow and lost. Her gray roots had grown, the rest of her hair dull and lifeless. She looked like a shell of her former self. Once the door closed behind us and I sat down across from her I found that I had no words.

She stared at the floor and then finally looked up at me. "This is a death penalty state and if I'm convicted I'll end up on death row. I'm going to die whether it's now or later. I figured I might as well have control over it."

"Sarah, the chief knows you didn't do this," I lied. "She's doing her best to find the real killer."

"You're just saying that to make me feel better. My lawyer even thinks I did it, even though he pretends not to."

"If that's true you need another lawyer. Do you have an alibi for the time of the shooting? That could help."

"I was home alone. Can't prove a thing."

"They found another set of prints on that gun and also found out how the person got into your house. They're matching prints as we speak. Do you know anyone who might have known about that weapon?"

"My family are the only ones aware of that gun and they're all dead." She stared into the distance, a look of recognition appearing on her face before she turned back. "Now that I think about it, I did show it to a man I dated. He seemed to know all about my grandfather and what he did in the war, where and how he died. He called him Private Cumberland. And he mentioned my father, Timothy, acted as though they were friends, but I knew that couldn't be. My father was killed before I was born. This guy was close to my age and there was something familiar about him, but I knew I'd never met him before. It was eerie, to tell you the truth."

"What was his name?"

"He told me his name was John Smith. We met in the oddest way—we literally ran into each other in the street. I asked him in for tea because he'd hurt his ankle when we collided." Her hands twisted together. "If what you say is true, why am I still here?"

"I don't know for sure, but I think it's because there's so much media coverage. The parents want justice, and things seem to have calmed down since you were arrested."

Sarah began to cry. "Oh great—they think I did it too."

I put my hand on her bone-thin wrist. "That's why it's safer for you to be here, at least until they find the person who actually did it."

Sarah looked up, her eyes bleak and filled with tears. "You think the parents would come after me?"

I shrugged. "The parents are crazed with grief, Sarah. Who knows what might happen? Can you be patient for a few more days? They'll find the killer and then give the news out to the media—after that you can safely go home."

The guard at the door signaled me and I stood up. "Will you promise me you won't harm yourself?"

Sarah nodded and then we hugged for a long moment. I left her there and followed the guard back to the chief's office.

"Well?" the chief asked as soon as I entered her office.

"She mentioned showing the gun to a man she dated a while back. His name was John Smith. I assured her that as soon as you find the real killer she'll be able to go home. I certainly hope that happens soon."

The chief shook her head. "So do I, but I can't guarantee anything. We'll look in the database for this John Smith, but if that's his real name and he hasn't committed a crime, he won't be there."

"She said he knew all about her grandfather and her father, even about where they were when they were killed. Where would he get that information?"

"I'll talk to her and get a description of this man, show her some mug shots. I would imagine her grandfather's service record is easy enough to obtain."

"Have you found anything at the house?"

She shook her head. "Thanks for coming in, Summer. I appreciate it. I'll let you know as soon as we have more news."

I left the station, my mind full of this mysterious John Smith, wondering what his part in this might be. Why would he be interested in her grandfather—Grant Cumberland was a minor player in the war and died in the line of duty. As far as I knew he had no claim to fame. I decided to go to the library and look up Private Grant Cumberland. It was within walking distance and since I hadn't heard from Jerry I figured he and Sam were still hard at it.

The library had nothing about Grant Cumberland other than some old articles about his marriage to Sadie and the two children they had—a boy and a girl. Two? I thought they'd only had Timothy, Sarah's father, who was also killed in the war. I called the chief on her private line. "I think Sarah's father had a sister," I told her. "You might want to look into her."

It was after seven when I left the library, and I'd still

had no call from

Jerry. I debated about whether to call or not, and decided no. I hailed a cab and had the East Indian man drop me off at home.

When I walked in the door Tom was sitting on my couch. He immediately stood, his hazel eyes searching my face.

"Are you ready to take me back?" he asked.

"Tom, I—"

"I'm sorry about the way I left last time. It was thoughtless—and then as the days went by I didn't have the nerve to face you. I kept wondering why you didn't ask me to stay, but then I realized you were angry with me. You aren't still angry, are you?"

"Tom—"

He bent his head, his hands going into fists. "I knew I should have come back sooner. We were a good couple, Summer. Can't we try again? My suitcase is out in the car. I don't expect to move in, just spend a day or two together in order to make-up."

"Jerry and I are back together."

His eyes went wide, his expression turning to one of disbelief. "What? I thought you hated him."

"There's a fine line—"

"Yeah, yeah, between love and hate. When did this happen and why didn't you call and tell me? Now I've made a fool of myself."

"No, you haven't. I should have called. It was very inconsiderate of me."

"I miss you, Summer—I was really hoping we—"

"I'm sorry, Tom."

His face suddenly contorted into an ugly mask of anger, an expression I'd never seen on it before. "You used me, didn't you? I was the idiot rebound and when

116

you got tired of me you just moved on."

"I can't help the timing of everything. Perhaps I did get together with you when I was still grieving, but I enjoyed being with you. Don't turn it into something ugly."

"It is ugly!" he shouted. "And you're a horrible bitch. Thanks for nothing." He opened the door and then turned and flung my house key on the floor. "Won't be needing that again," he muttered. He slammed the door so hard a light dusting of plaster loosened and sifted onto the rug.

I sat on the loveseat for a long time going over what Tom had said. I had been callous, but his incessant mothering had finally driven me round the bend. I didn't need a parent, I wanted a lover and a companion.

14

Jerry didn't return that night or the next one, and by the second morning I was frantic with worry. When I called his cell it went straight to voice mail. I almost called Agnes but decided not to worry her. I made my espresso in a daze and fed Mischief and Cutty who seemed to know how upset I was, huddling around my legs and tripping me more than once.

The scene with Tom haunted me, making me feel like a jerk for not letting him know, but he hadn't called me either. It seemed strange for him to show up in my house after all this time. If I really thought about it, I guess I had used him to get over Jerry—but I hadn't known it at the time. Sometimes life was like that, punching you in the stomach when you least expected it. I'd had my share of it a few years back and it had taken me months to get back on my feet. I understood how he felt.

It was raining when I left the house for the shop and I carried an umbrella, hurrying down the slippery sidewalk toward the other end of town. No one was about and I began to wonder if something else strange had happened, but when I ran into Marguerite Powers, from the apartments across from the market, she had nothing to report. "You did well," she whispered, glancing left and right. "The healing worked."

Yes, but who had it worked for? Apparently not the

parents who still crowded around the police station hoping they could lynch the person responsible for their child's death. We smiled and waved as she crossed the street, heading to do her food shopping.

When I arrived at the shop there were several people standing outside, two with signs that read DEVIL WORSHIPPER. I had never seen these women and wondered where they'd come from. They stared at me with looks of pure hatred showing me the back of their signs that read: BOYCOTT THIS SHOP!

I hurried past and opened up, closing the door and locking it behind me. After opening the register I called Jerry's cell again, but it still went to voice mail. Finally I called the chief on the pretense of finding out about Sarah, but after chatting for a minute or two I realized she knew nothing about Jerry. Apparently he and Sam had taken a couple of days off, which was news to me.

Sandra told me that Sarah was the same, and she had discovered zilch about Timothy's missing sister.

"Did you ask Sarah if she remembers an aunt?"

"I did, but she didn't seem to know much. Her mother didn't talk at all about her husband's family while Sarah was growing up. According to Sarah her mother got pregnant when her father was home on leave and he was killed not long after he went back. Sarah never even met Timothy Cumberland."

"How do we trace her?"

"I have a team on it, Summer," she said, dismissively.

In other words leave it for the experts? When I told her about the picketers outside my store there was silence for a moment. Finally she said, "I'll send a uniform down to get rid of them."

I was happy to hear this since I had a feeling many of my customers would be scared away by these dour women wearing black with heavy crosses around their necks. Once I hung up I thought again about Sarah. Was media pressure causing the chief to abandon her principles?

A police car rolled up fifteen minutes later and two cops got out. They spoke with them and then the two women gave up their posts and walked away, the others trailing along behind them. After they left my customers trickled in, the day seeming to stretch into two. I was distracted about the picketers and Jerry, worried about Sarah, my mind whirling in every direction as I tried to make change and deal with purchases.

At noon I decided to go over and talk to Becky at Daily Bread and find out more about her trance-like statement from the other day. If the chief wasn't going to pursue other avenues I felt obliged to look into things myself. "Would you mind watching the shop while I run over to Daily Bread?" I asked Douglas.

"I'd be happy to," he said, looking around at the two other people in the store. "What do I do if they want to purchase something?"

"Tell them cash only. I won't be long." I hurried out the door and jogged down the sidewalk toward Daily Bread.

Becky was standing behind the long counter, wisps of hair pulling free of her braid, her face flushed from the heat of the ovens. "Do you need some sustenance?" she asked, smiling.

I smiled and shook my head. "Becky, when you were in my shop a while back you said something about the woods west of town, or at least that's what I thought you were talking about. I think that's where the meth lab is, but I had the feeling you weren't referring to that. Do you remember?"

Becky shook her head, her eyes darting to the one customer coming toward the counter with a loaf of bread. "Wait one second," she said, turning to help the woman with her purchase. After the woman left Becky turned to me. "Now, what were you saying?"

I went through the whole thing again, watching Becky's eyes glaze over.

She nodded as though she was seeing something I couldn't see. "It's there but doesn't want to be found," she said in a monotone.

"What is it?"

Becky shook herself. "What is what?"

"You were in a trance again, but what you said is very enigmatic. I wish you could be more specific."

"What did I say?"

"You said: *it's there but it doesn't want to be found.*"

"Hmm," Becky said, grinning. "That is a little vague, isn't it? Wish I could help you but I'm kind of busy." She nodded to a man who had just arrived.

"Should we comb the woods?" I asked.

Becky looked perplexed, her thick brows pulling together. "How would I know?"

"Oh Becky, you're impossible. Will you come with me?"

"I don't think I'd be much help," she said, taking money from the man and ringing him up. "Half the time what I say in that state turns out to be wrong."

"But what about the other half?" I hissed, making sure the customer didn't hear.

I hurried out the door, nearly tripping in my haste to get back to Tarot and Tea. Talking to Becky had made me anxious to get the police to search the woods, but there were acres and acres out there. Would the chief search again on the strength of what my psychic friend had said? I was already pushing things with Sadie's ghost. I sighed and called her number.

"Can you get some guys to search the woods again?" I asked when she answered.

"What now, Summer? Have you spoken to a real person or is this more hearsay from Sadie?"

"I heard it from Becky who goes into trance from time to time—she said and I quote, *there is something out there.*

Sandra Marshall laughed. "Of course there's something out there—miles and miles of woods and an abandoned shack where the meth lab was."

"I know it sounds far-fetched, but—"

Sandra Marshall interrupted, her tone less than cordial. "Please don't call me with this sort of nonsense, Summer. I gave in about Sadie, against my better judgment, but this is going too far. I need real evidence now."

"What would it hurt to send a couple of—?"

"I don't have men to spare right now."

I was about to answer when I heard the click of the call ending. Maybe Sam and Jerry had discovered something. If they hadn't I would have to go out there by myself.

By the time five o'clock rolled around I was feeling hollow-eyed and dazed, my mind fixated on Sarah and how to prove her innocence. My cell phone rang just as I was leaving the shop, shocking my wayward thoughts into the present. "Summer, have you heard from Sam or Jerry?"

"No, Agnes. I've tried to call Jerry but he isn't

answering."

"Sam told me they were tracking Cable and his buddies, but it's been two full days. I'm freaking out."

"Me too, but I don't know what we can do about it."

"We could call the police station and report it to the chief."

I thought about that for a moment—after my last conversation with her I didn't think she'd be happy to hear from me again. "What would we say?"

"Tell her the truth—they went to track them and haven't called in. I think that's enough."

"Will you call? I have a feeling the chief will take what you say more seriously. Here's her private cell number." I rattled off the numbers knowing that Agnes would remember them.

"I'm calling right now—I'll let you know what she says."

The phone rang ten minutes later. "She was livid, Summer! I think she's madder about them disobeying her than the fact that they're missing."

"Is she going to do anything about it?"

"No. Her entire reaction was annoyance. She said they had no business going off on their own and that she had half a mind to lay them both off. I'm totally panicking right now."

"I'd come over if I had a car. I'm walking right now."

"I'll be there by the time you get home. Open the wine."

"But Agnes, you—" I heard the click of the line and knew she'd hung up.

Had she forgotten she was pregnant? I jogged the remaining mile, hurrying inside to check my e-mail before she arrived. Maybe Jerry had left me a message.

But there was no message.

Agnes arrived ten minutes later, screeching to a halt in front of my cottage. She got out of the car, pushed her hair back off her face in a nervous gesture I'd never seen her use and hurried to the front door. When I opened the door she was standing there staring into space.

"Why hasn't he called?" she cried, her eyes filling. "I'm really scared,

Summer. If something happens to Sam, I don't know what—"

I took her by the arm and led her into the kitchen. "Try and calm down,

Agnes. They might be out of range, you know. The cell reception around here is spotty at best."

Agnes stared at me and then pointed to the bottle of wine I'd opened.

"Can I have a glass? I know I'm not supposed to drink, but in these circumstances I think it might help. I promise I won't have much."

I poured her half a glass and handed it over and then poured one for myself. It was a low alcohol red I'd found recently so I didn't feel bad about giving her to her. We sat in the living room without talking until her cell phone rang, muffled inside her leather bag in the kitchen. When she jumped up, her wine spilled down her black shirt and pooled on the carpet, reminding me of blood.

"Hello?" she said breathlessly. "Is that you, Sam—I can barely hear you.

Where are you?"

A moment went by and then another as Agnes stood there with her phone pressed to her ear. "Are you and Jerry all right?"

I hurried into the kitchen. "Let me talk to Jerry," I

whispered, holding out my hand. She stared at me and shook her head.

"Okay. Okay. I'll see you when you get back." She pressed end and slid her phone into her purse. "They're okay and on their way back."

"What else did he say? Where are they?"

"They're in some small town on the western side of Connecticut, but I couldn't get the name. I guess they're bringing Cable in. The rest of the guys got away."

I headed into the pantry to find some soda to put on the stain, wondering if Cable could be our killer. I doubted it, but I couldn't say why. Once I'd cleaned up the wine Agnes was putting on her coat.

"I want to be home when he gets there," she told me giving me a hug. "I can't tell you how relieved I am."

It was two and a half hours later before I heard Jerry's motorcycle coming down the road. I flung the door open and was standing at the curb when he rolled up and cut the engine. "What happened out there?" I asked.

He stepped off the bike, pulled his helmet off and took me in his arms.

"Jesus, I'm glad to be here," he whispered into my hair. His hands were on my back pulling me closer when I saw my busybody neighbor, Betty Franklin, peering at us from behind her living room curtain.

"We'd better take this inside," I whispered, pulling away. I nodded toward where I could see her in the light from the streetlamp. I led the way inside and closed the door, turning to him again. And this time there was no hesitation when our lips met.

When we finally pulled apart he looked dazed. "It was a shit storm out there. I wondered if we'd make it back."

"Why didn't Al and that other guy go with you?"

Jerry shook his head and ran his fingers through his hair. "I didn't want to get them in trouble. Sam and I figured we'd could handle it on our own—to tell you the truth we didn't think we'd find them." He met my gaze, his eyes hollow and bloodshot from lack of sleep. "When we took Cable in to the station the chief was waiting for us. I could be fired."

"What? For bringing in a suspect in the shooting?"

"Sam and I didn't follow proper police procedure and we went behind her back. My mother has decided to wage war against her."

Jerry's mother had been a thorn in our side from day one, expecting Jerry to move in with her after Jerry's father's suicide. Jerry still felt responsible for her. I wondered if her name had come up during his therapy. If it hadn't it should have. "When did you see your mom?"

Jerry looked embarrassed for a moment. "I went by before I came here—she left six messages on my phone. I was afraid something had happened."

"I won't even ask," I muttered. "Did you tell her we were seeing each other?"

"No. I wasn't ready to hear her litany of reasons why it wasn't a good idea. But I did tell her about the chief's reaction to what we did—her warning. Mom has little tolerance for Sandra Marshall, thinks my father was a much better chief."

"Even though he was dirty?"

Jerry scoffed. "Since his death she's put him on a pedestal. It's like all that stuff he did never happened."

"Now tell me all about this 'caper' you managed to pull off."

"Can I have a glass of wine first?" he asked, heading into the kitchen. He pulled the cork out of the bottle and retrieved a glass from the cupboard, pouring a sizable amount into the water glass. "And I'd like to take a long hot bath. I haven't showered in two days."

I cocked my head and looked up at him. "Does the bath include company?"

He grinned. "I need someone to wash my back." He lifted one eyebrow. "And maybe other parts as well?"

"Jerry!" I scolded, laughing. I knew all of this was a diversion so he didn't have to tell me the horror of what had gone on. I could wait, especially since what he had in mind for tonight was so inviting. Tomorrow was soon enough to hear all the lurid details.

15

In the morning Jerry and I had coffee together before we each took off for work. I told him I wanted to walk since the weather was pleasant, watching him get on his bike and roar away in the other direction. The day went by quickly, the store filled with customers looking for talismans and books about life after death, as well as ways in which to contact the spirit world. I recognized some of these women, knowing they had lost their children. I hoped that their purchases would bring them some modicum of peace. I was glad to see that at least some townspeople appreciated what Tarot and Tea had to offer and didn't think I was the devil's spawn.

After they left I spent time looking through catalogues to reorder the things I'd lost, poring over new improved essential oil dispensers and Tarot and goddess card sets that had just come out. My bank account had dwindled in recent weeks and the loss of so much stock had made matters worse. I didn't think the insurance I carried would pay for what was destroyed.

When I arrived home Jerry was on the loveseat, a beer in his hand. He hadn't shaved and with his Italian heritage this meant that he had more than a five-o'clock shadow and looked very scruffy. "What's going on? Is the chief giving you a day off?"

Jerry frowned, rubbing a hand across his chin. "I'm

off duty for a month. She seems to think that what Sam and I did was so terrible that I needed to be punished, even though we brought the bastard in."

I went to the kitchen and poured myself a glass of wine. "An entire month? That seems unduly harsh," I said, joining him in the living room. "Did she tell you this today?" I asked, sitting beside him.

Jerry stared at the floor. "She told me yesterday before I left."

"Where were you going this morning?"

"I had an appointment with the therapist. I didn't tell you because I didn't want to worry you."

"Jerry, we need to have an agreement not to keep secrets. If we're together then we share everything, good and bad, okay?"

Jerry nodded, his gaze sliding away. "The chief also said that if I didn't get my shit together I'd be fired. All Sam got was a slap on the wrist."

"What happened with him?"

"He's on desk duty until his shoulder is fully healed."

"Shoulder? Was he shot?"

Jerry gazed at me. "I didn't tell you? Yeah, he was shot—I took him to the hospital right after we dropped Cable off."

"And you went to your mom's after that? No wonder it took so long for you to get here." I took a sip of wine, thinking about Jerry keeping all of this to himself. He was very adept at compartmentalizing. "The chief has to know that being with those meth-heads for so long stressed you out—not to mention the drugs. She needs to give you a break."

"Tell me about it. I haven't felt this bad since—" He glanced at me and then away. "I think she thinks I'm still on drugs—she told me I had to see Cynthia at least once a week for the next month."

"Are you ready to tell me about what went down out there and how you managed to capture Cable?"

Jerry nodded slowly and put his beer down on the coffee table. He turned to me and began to talk in a monotone, indicating his state of mind.

"We were able to follow them from the tire tracks they left in the mud in the woods and then by the crap they threw out the windows—what a bunch of pigs. We found some of their equipment by the side of the road as well as candy wrappers and beer cans. I guess they just tossed it out as they drove so that if they got caught they wouldn't have any evidence on them. I handed it all in for DNA but don't know whether the chief will bother with it or not."

He picked up his beer and took a long pull, his dark eyes meeting mine. "We found them in Oakville. They were holed up in a motel on the edge of town. When Sam and I came through the door two of them went out the back window. The other two shot at us and Sam was hit in the shoulder. Luckily I moved away in time. But when Sam went down the other two ran by us out the front door and disappeared. It was Sam who told me that Cable was in the next room. I cornered him and he threw down his weapon. You know the rest."

"And Sam's okay?"

"He may have to wear a sling for the wedding, but other than that he's fine. Luckily the bullet missed anything important and went straight through. The guy has an angel on his shoulder."

"Agnes was really worried."

Jerry gazed at me, his brows furrowed. "I found out that one of those druggies is the chief's nephew. No wonder she warned them to get out of there. I think the entire reason she had me holed up with them was to keep an eye on the dude."

"But you didn't know who he was."

"I only know now because Cable told us on the way to the police station. He also talked about some homeless dude living up there in the woods. According to Cable the guy's a survivalist or something. I'm not sure whether to believe him since he could be telling me this to get himself off the suspect list."

I was still caught up in the nephew bit, my thoughts going back to my last conversation with the chief. "Will the chief face charges for warning those guys? Seems like she could get into trouble for that."

"If Sam or I happened to take this to the DA she might, but she's our chief."

"Do you trust her? I don't see her looking for the real killer."

"She's questioning Cable, and believe me, she'll get the truth out of him. I think she's convinced that Sarah did it, especially with the gun and the prints. She's determined to close the case sooner rather than later."

"I forgot to tell you—Becky, you know my friend who goes into trances every so often? She had one about the woods. I think the killer could be up there. Maybe he's the guy Cable was talking about."

"I wouldn't put much stock in anything Cable said. Sam and I combed through several acres and didn't come across anything. There's more than fifty acres of woods on the outskirts of town."

"I have a feeling it's close to where Cable and those guys had their lab."

"That's where we went." He stared at me. "Are you suggesting I take you out there?"

"Maybe."

Jerry gazed into space for a long moment before turning back to me. "Can you take tomorrow off? I think whoever might have been there is long gone, but it wouldn't hurt to take another look—and I have nothing better to do," he added with a grimace. "Maybe we'll get lucky and find a campsite or something."

"Will you get in trouble if the chief finds out?"

Jerry made a sound in the back of his throat. "What do I have to lose? According to her I have to see the therapist at least four times before she'll consider reinstating me. Thank god she didn't take away my badge and my gun."

He smiled but I had a feeling he wasn't smiling inside. I thought about the two of us sleuthing together, something we'd enjoyed in the past. And in the mood he was in I thought it might do him some good to get out of the house. I knew Becky's words meant something, despite her telling me she was only right half of the time. There was magic in her, I'd tasted it in the bread she made, seen it evidenced by the people who lined up outside her bakery.

"Maybe I could get someone to watch the store."

"Call Agnes. Sam says she's about to go nuts about the wedding. She could use a distraction for a day."

When I dialed Agnes's number she didn't even say hello, her voice shrill and upset. "I guess you know that Sam got shot? He could have been killed."

"I know that, Agnes. He's a cop."

"I want him to quit the force—I go crazy with worry every time something like this happens."

"You knew what he did for a living when you met him. Sam is dedicated to his work, just as Jerry is. I would never ask Jerry to quit."

"Is it true what Sam told me about Jerry, that's he on unofficial leave?"

I glanced at Jerry. "Yes, and he's very unhappy about it. He has a month to dwell on the possibility of being fired."

"Is this all because they went off on their own? I wish she'd told Sam he had to take a month off."

"No you don't. He'd go crazy, and besides you have a couple of weeks set aside for your honeymoon, don't you?"

"That's the other thing—he's wearing a sling and our wedding is coming up way too soon."

"Try and look at the bright side—you guys are going to the Bahamas for a vacation right afterward."

"The arm is keeping us from—you know."

"It will be all healed by the time you go, and I'm sure you can find some creative ways around it."

Agnes giggled. "I tried but all it did was make us laugh."

"Laughing's good. I wish Jerry was laughing." When I looked over at him, he made a face.

"Sam said they questioned Cable. I sure hope they let that poor woman out of jail soon."

"I do too. The reason I called is to ask you if you'd mind watching the shop tomorrow."

Agnes laughed. "And what are you and Jerry planning to do?"

"Not what you think. Can you?"

"Sure, why not? Anything I need to know?"

"Nothing new. Thanks Agnes."

Jerry rose from the chair and came toward me with a look on his face that I knew only too well. "What— *now*?"

"I need you, Summer, especially after this latest

shitty news. It's been ten long months of nothing."

I stared at him. "Are you telling me you didn't have sex for the entire time we were apart?"

"That's what I'm saying. Believe it or not, it's the truth."

I was so taken aback that I couldn't speak for a moment. I'd dated Tom for several months and had assumed Jerry was dating too. For someone like him, abstinence was unheard of. "Why?" I finally asked.

Jerry frowned, his brown eyes troubled. "I had a breakdown, Summer. I thought you knew."

"I knew you were having a hard time, but—"

"You thought it was business as usual and that I'd just jump into bed with another woman? I'm surprised Sam didn't fill you in. It was four long months before the chief let me back on the force and even then I was on probation. This last thing with Cable may be the end of my career. She doesn't do well with cops taking matters into their own hands."

I sat at the kitchen table. "Are you serious?"

Jerry pulled out a chair and sat next to me. "I'm about as serious as I can get. If she throws me off the force there's nothing left for me. Being a cop is my entire life."

"I know that. And you've worked hard to get your head together. What if Cable is the killer or we find something out in the woods—won't that get her to relent?"

"Since talking to him I don't think he's the killer, but he's still guilty of being part of a gang who makes and sells meth. I'm glad he's behind bars. And now we'll get the others because he'll cop a plea and give them up."

"But not her nephew."

Jerry scoffed. "The chief already rescued her nephew

and put him into rehab somewhere."

"Who told you that?"

"Sam. And she swore him to secrecy. I'm not supposed to know."

"I'll go with you to Cynthia if you'd like. This thing with Jim keeps coming up in my mind and I'm afraid it's going to affect our relationship."

"That might be a good idea. I remember you saying that you'd do whatever the therapist suggested."

"Just let me know when. This latest suspension could put you into an emotional tailspin."

Jerry nodded. "Tell me about it—the chief doesn't realize how much I count on my job."

"Or she does know and doesn't much care. I'm beginning to dislike her."

When I reached to give him a hug, his head came down on my shoulder, his lips brushing my ear. "Being here with you helps," he whispered. "I'd be a gibbering idiot right now if we hadn't gotten back together."

I pulled away but held on to his arms. "Let's concentrate on getting you back in her good graces. If we don't find anything in the woods I suggest you lay low for a while. There's no point in pissing her off further."

Jerry kissed me after that, and then pulled me to my feet. I followed him into the bedroom. With his arms tight around me I could let go of the rising anxiety about the case and Jerry's depression. When he said breakdown it meant he'd been unable to cope *at all* for four months. I wondered if he might be on anti-depressants, but so far I hadn't seen a pill bottle in the bathroom. I couldn't believe the chief had laid him off for an entire month. Jerry would surely lose it with so much time on his hands.

16

Jerry and I headed out early, taking a circuitous back road toward the woods and the area where the meth lab had been. It was cloudy and looked like rain and I hoped it would wait until we got home. I didn't much like the idea of being on the back of Jerry's motorcycle in a rainstorm, nor did I care to traipse around the woods getting my boots muddy and wet.

We parked the bike along a dirt pullout and then Jerry led the way along a narrow animal trail. "The meth-lab's about a mile up. I figured we could start there."

"But you and Sam already went over a lot of territory, didn't you?" I asked, running to catch up.

"We checked the immediate area close to the meth-lab because Cable said the guy took pot-shots at them. Aside from the trampled grass around the shack, we didn't find any sign of broken branches or footprints or anything to suggest another person was living up here. Hope we'll be luckier today."

I didn't say anything as I followed him deeper into the woods. When we came to an abandoned wooden shack that looked about to fall down I knew it was where the lab had been. He gave it a wide berth and headed northwest, bush whacking through the thick weeds and bushes that filled in the shadows beneath the tightly packed trees. There were ash, oaks and maples and some pines here, dogwood and hazel in between. Once spring really sprung this area would be filled with the creamy white of dogwood blossoms.

Jerry stopped and turned, his finger to his lips. "Did you hear something?" he whispered.

"No," I whispered back. "Just birds and chipmunks."

Jerry nodded and moved forward again. It was close to an hour of walking before he stopped again. "There's something over there," he said moving to the right.

I followed him into a clearing where he reached down and picked a can out from under the mat of damp leaves. "This has been here for a while," he said, holding it out to me.

When I took it from him I felt a tingle in my fingers. The rusted-out can had been filled with beans, a staple of anyone living in the woods. As soon as I put it on the ground my hands stopped tingling. But then I felt a strange pull in my solar plexus and headed away from where Jerry still searched, following my instincts deeper into the forest. I climbed a rocky hill, on the lookout for anything unusual. I heard Jerry crashing through the trees behind me, surprised at how much noise he was making, but when I turned it was not Jerry. It was a misty translucent image of a man who looked to be in his fifties, brown hair pushed back from a wide forehead, his perceptive gaze on me. We locked eyes for a long moment.

When Jerry appeared a second later the apparition disappeared. "I think I just saw a ghost," I told him, pointing toward the spot where he'd been.

"What? Who was it?"

I shrugged. "Something led me up here—maybe him. Let's take a look around." I began to search the area methodically, being careful not to disturb whatever might be hidden under the mossy undergrowth.

"Found something," Jerry said from a distance on my left.

When I reached him he was standing close to a small hollow next to an enormous moss-covered tree. When he pointed into the leafy detritus and then bent down I moved closer, kneeling next to him. Under the leaves I could see what looked like yellowed newspaper clippings. I pulled one out, holding it in the shaft of dim light that slanted through the thick foliage. "This looks really old." I tried to read it as Jerry dug further, coming up with a weathered black notebook and a battered army issue canteen that seemed to date back to the Second World War.

"Jerry, this article is the original obituary for Grant Cumberland. It says he died on April 19th, 1944." I handed him the piece of brittle paper.

"Looks like there are more newspaper articles, Summer. Can you fish them out of there while I read this?"

I dug around under the leaves and found several more articles that discussed the school being turned over to the army and what this meant for the town of Ames. Apparently there had been an uproar about it, many residents upset about so many of their young men being called up to fight. Another yellowed strip was the obit for Sadie Cumberland. Apparently she had one survivor— Lucille Cumberland.

"Why are these here?" Jerry asked, a puzzled look on his face, "and how, after all these years of wind and rain and snow, did they survive?"

"Maybe they were kept safe. Maybe whoever had these is our killer."

Jerry opened the notebook, his brows furrowing as he attempted to read it. "This is someone's journal." He handed it to me. "It's not easy to make out the writing."

I took it from him. *Today is the day my father died,*" I read out loud. *And if they had their way I would be dead too. I suppose I could be called crazy, but under the circumstances I don't feel that way about it. I will get even, mark my words. No one gets to obliterate my life like that.*

The rest of the pages had been smeared and the ink had run. I couldn't read any further.

"That doesn't help much," Jerry said. "I wish it hadn't been rained on. Is there a date at least?"

I examined the pages again. "I don't see any."

Jerry moved leaves aside carefully checking for any more evidence left behind. He pulled out the remnants of a plaid jacket. "Someone lived here for a while," he finally said, standing. "Maybe we'll get lucky and find some DNA, but I doubt it. It's been here too long."

I moved around the tree, kicking leaves and detritus aside as I went. When my toe came against something hard I bent down to find out what it was. "Look at this," I called, holding up a very old handgun.

Jerry pulled gloves out of his pocket, put them on and then took the weapon from me, depositing it into a plastic bag. "This could be all we need," he said, his eyes unreadable.

He handed me another plastic bag and I carefully put in the newspaper articles, hoping the paper would hold together at least until the chief could take a look.

Jerry glanced at me. "I don't have a bag big enough for the jacket so I guess we'll have to carry it."

"What made you decide to bring the evidence bags along?"

"What self-respecting cop goes anywhere without a

few evidence bags? Especially when they're searching for evidence." Jerry smirked and pulled his jacket back. "I have my weapon along too."

I made a small sound in the back of my throat. "Glad you came prepared. I figured since you and Sam already searched we wouldn't find anything out here."

"We wouldn't have found this if you hadn't followed your instincts to this particular spot, my little witchy woman." He grinned. "Let's get this back to the chief. Maybe she'll be lenient on me once she sees what we found. I think that dude is out here somewhere, but I don't want to search for him with you along. Maybe the chief will let Sam and me come back later."

I didn't answer but I had my doubts about Sandra Marshall allowing Jerry anywhere near the woods. She was on Jerry's case and one more instance of insubordination could spell disaster. I hoped my involvement would soften her response to our evidence-gathering.

On the way back to the bike I heard frenzied barking. When some shots rang out in the distance Jerry grabbed my arm. "We've got to get out of here before those wackos mistake us for deer."

"Is that why they're out here? I've heard townspeople talking about cults and devil worshipers. I guess Sarah being behind bars isn't enough for them."

Jerry met my gaze. "I wish I hadn't been suspended—this could turn ugly."

"It already is," I said, thinking about the couples in my store, the signs of distrust and hysteria I'd already witnessed.

It began to rain on the ride back and by the time we reached the station I was shivering, my jeans drenched.

"Why didn't we think to take rain gear?" I asked Jerry petulantly.

He helped me off the bike. "Nothing like a little hardship to make what we found all the more sweet." He picked up the plaid jacket and headed inside and I hurried after him, the plastic bags in my hands.

We were sitting in the chief's office waiting for her when Sam stuck his head in the door. "You found something?"

Jerry nodded, his gaze going to me. "Glad I took my ghost buster along," he whispered. "A ghost out there showed her where to go. We may have the killer if we can track him."

Sam raised his eyebrows. "Track the ghost or the shooter?"

Jerry was just about to answer when the chief pushed past Sam and closed the door in his face. "What are you up to now, Jerry Brady? I thought I told you to see Cynthia and stay out of police business."

Jerry glanced toward me before settling his gaze on Sandra Marshall. "We found evidence in the woods that points to someone living out there. Did Cable mention this when you questioned him? He told me a story about a person taking pots shots at the lab, but at the time I chalked it up to him trying to cover his butt. It could be our killer."

Sandra Marshall stood in front of us, her arms crossed. "Cable was more than willing to give up every name of his group, but he didn't mention another man living up there."

Jerry gestured for me to hand over my bags and then held out the jacket. "If we can get DNA off this stuff we should be able to ID him. And the gun must have some prints left on it. Unfortunately it's been out there for a while."

The chief took the bags and put them down on her desk. She frowned, her narrowed gaze going from Jerry to me. "I don't see how this can have any relevance to the case. From what I can see these newspaper articles are ancient and the gun is too." She picked up the bag and studied it. "This is a Colt 45—as old as the hills. It was probably left behind by some homeless guy who stole it years ago."

"But you will check it for prints, right?"

The chief shook her head in an irritated way. "You are really trying my patience. We have our shooter in a cell downstairs."

"Sarah didn't do it," I blurted. "You have to at least have all of this checked out."

She cast an unfriendly look my way and turned back to Jerry. "And where is the shooter, Jerry? All this stuff does is confuse the issue. The case is going to trial in a month and a half. Sarah has been arraigned and no one came forward to post her bail."

"And Jim Salazar was working for the prosecuting attorney and nearly raped me," I said, staring up at her.

"Jim Salazar is being punished for what he did, but that has nothing to do with the case."

"Except that he pretended to be someone he wasn't," I said.

The chief scoffed. "You think that doesn't happen every day with cases like this? It's the way business is conducted. How else could he find out what the defense has up its sleeve?"

"He should never have targeted Summer," Jerry said, his eyes narrowing. "Bringing her in for interrogatories is one thing, but this was underhanded."

The chief stared at him. "Jerry, you've been

suspended and the fact that you are still pursuing this case when I asked you specifically not to, makes me think I should kick you off the force for good."

Jerry's normally olive skin turned sallow. "Summer and I are trying to—"

"I know exactly why you did what you did, but that doesn't make it right. I'll have the ME take a look but don't expect much to come from it. And please, Jerry, stay out of this? I really don't want to fire you." She smiled for the first time and moved to sit down at her desk, her attention going to a stack of papers.

On our way out I saw Sam in the back talking to another cop. I was going to call out goodbye, but Jerry took hold of my hand and dragged me out of the station.

Once we were outside he turned to me. "Glad she's sending it all down to the medical examiner. I was afraid she was going to throw us out and the evidence along with us."

"When do you think he'll know anything?"

"A day, maybe two? Depends on his workload. I'll call him first thing tomorrow and check on what he found."

"What about the chief?"

"Screw the chief—if she thinks I'm going to stand idly by while Sarah gets thrown in prison for a crime she didn't commit, she's got another thing coming."

I laughed. "Okay. Let's talk about those newspaper articles and see what we can come up with. There's a reason they were out there. What do you think we should do next?"

"Once I talk to Ray I'll let you know."

Jerry handed me my helmet but I didn't put it on, my mind still on the newspaper clippings. "Those articles mentioned the sister, Lucille. Maybe if we can find her we can get closer to figuring out what's going on. Someone had those articles for a reason. Whoever owns that Colt could be the killer."

Jerry pulled on his helmet. "Whoever was out there is either long gone, dead, or hiding somewhere. Just because he had that Colt doesn't mean he shot up the school with the Tommy gun. Ray will know if that gun's been fired recently. That could help."

"I know it isn't the weapon he used at the school. My question is, if this is the shooter, why did he shoot all those kids and then take the gun back to Sarah's house?"

Jerry climbed on and started the bike. "Good question. If he is the shooter why didn't just leave that old Thompson out in the woods somewhere? And what's his motive?"

"He sounded upset in that one journal entry, like someone screwed him over. But who?"

Jerry shrugged and revved the bike. "Get on."

I looked up at the darkening sky, realizing how late it was. It looked like another night of rain was heading our way. "Where are we going?"

"Home. We have an early appointment with Cynthia tomorrow."

"But what about my work?"

"The appointment is at seven-thirty. I think you'll make it on time."

I climbed on behind him wondering when he'd called the therapist. The only time we'd been apart was when he went to the men's room at the police station.

I put my arms around his waist, leaned my head against his back and we took off with a roar and a cloud of black smoke.

17

Jerry and I sat next to one another on a small couch in a room that looked like it belonged in *Architectural Digest*. The furniture was obviously very expensive, with two Chinese chests in red tones and thick cream-colored carpet on the floor. Cynthia Blackwell, a stunning woman in her forties, wore an off-white silk blouse that seemed to match the carpet, her thick blonde hair pulled back and fastened at the nape of her neck. Her make-up was perfect, her faintly lined brown eyes scrutinizing us from under brows that had been tastefully penciled in.

Cynthia crossed her perfectly shaped legs, one hand going to her hair, pushing in a wisp that had come out of her French twist. "So, Jerry, tell me why you are here and why you have brought Ms McCloud along."

Jerry flinched. "I'm here because the chief said I had to come. As far as Summer, she asked if she could come along."

"I'm not scolding you, Jerry. I only want to know what it is you expect to get out of today's session."

Jerry turned to me. "I guess we want to know how you feel about us being together again—whether you think it's too soon for us."

Cynthia smiled. "What do *you* think? That's what's important here. You've been in a very dark place for a long time and I would imagine that Summer is a bright spot in your current world. Isn't that so?"

Jerry glanced at me and then toward the therapist. "That is definitely so," he said, picking up my hand.

Her gaze moved to me. "I'm glad to meet you, Ms McCloud. Jerry's past sessions have often centered around your relationship. It's nice to have a face to go with the name." She smiled. "Jerry and I have spoken of what happened ten months ago and I also know that he's taken my advice and talked with you about his feelings. How do you feel about his presence in your life?"

I stared into her eyes, feeling inadequate. I had on jeans and a sweatshirt, my hair in tangles from neglecting to wear my helmet on the ten-minute ride on the motorcycle. "Please call me Summer." I glanced at Jerry who was watching me with a hopeful expression. "I love Jerry, but I am concerned that things are moving too fast. We've been apart for a long time and my trust was severely eroded by what happened between us. I don't want to wake up one morning and have him gone again. I guess that's my main worry."

Cynthia nodded and turned to Jerry. "Did you hear what Summer said, Jerry? What is your response to that?"

Jerry looked like a deer in the headlights for a moment. He ran nervous fingers through his thick hair and glanced quickly at me before focusing on Cynthia. "I can't guarantee anything. How do I know what the future holds?"

"I think what Summer is trying to say is that you need to have some parameters. For instance, not keeping secrets. I think Summer would feel better if she knew when you were feeling stressed, because stress is what led to your breakdown, and that breakdown is what caused you to disappear from her life. Both of you need to be able to talk about uncomfortable matters—allowing yourself to be vulnerable is the key to a good relationship."

"I don't like feeling vulnerable," Jerry said, his gaze on the rug.

"I understand, but unfortunately vulnerability is a reality of life. Without that there is no love."

"I blamed Jerry's breakdown on his feelings about the last case," I interjected. "He seemed to think he had nothing to do with solving it, but that wasn't true."

Cynthia leaned toward Jerry. "What do you think, Jerry? We've certainly covered all this in our months together."

Jerry looked up at Cynthia and turned to me. "With Cynthia's relentless digging I came to the conclusion that the breakdown was about Pop and my buried feelings. His lack of integrity affected me a lot more than I ever knew."

I stared at him. "So our break-up and the fact that I didn't hear from you wasn't about our case?"

Jerry nodded. "Pop always told me to tell the truth and especially when I decided to join the police force. Discovering that he was on the take and that he killed a man in order to cover it up blew my world apart." He glanced back at Cynthia. "But I didn't know it until I hit rock bottom."

There was a moment of silence and then Cynthia asked, "What have you both learned over the ten months you've been apart?"

Jerry and I looked at each other and then I said, "We learned that we love each other and that we make a good team."

Jerry said, "I learned that I'd rather be with Summer than alone."

"So, 'being with Summer rather than alone'—I would hope you've grown to love the inner part of you that you rejected."

Jerry sighed, his gaze going to the floor. "I am not enjoying this, Cynthia. And I don't like parsing my relationship with Summer. It really is none of your business."

I looked at Cynthia to see how she took this last statement, not surprised to see a hint of color appear on her cheekbones.

"Why did you bring her in if not to discuss your relationship?" the therapist finally asked.

"We're together now and I guess I wanted your blessing. I don't always state my feelings very well, but I do love Summer, and I hope we can make another go of it."

Cynthia nodded, her long fingers pushing another wayward wisp of hair back into the configuration at the back of her neck. "I think you have a good chance as long as you're honest with each other. The breakdown was no small matter, Jerry. I thought long and hard about whether you should be in a facility. In the end I decided to give you a chance on your own and only hoped that the anti-depressants combined with our therapy would get you through. Have you told this young woman the extent of what you went through?"

Jerry's troubled gaze met mine. "No, I guess not."

"Don't you think that would be a good idea?"

Jerry nodded, looking chastised. "I didn't want to burden her."

"This is a good example of what I've been trying to say—both of you need to be upfront about your feelings." Cynthia looked at her watch and rose. "Our time is up. Your homework, Jerry, is to explain what happened ten months ago. Let Summer decide if she wants to hear it or not."

"I do want to hear it," I said, turning to Jerry.

"Good. Shall we say next week at the same time?"

"With or without Summer?" Jerry asked, standing.

"Whatever you feel is best." Cynthia opened the door and ushered us out.

"I like her," I said once we were outside.

Jerry grimaced. "She doesn't give me a break."

"That's her job, Jerry. She's pushing you to do what's best for both of us."

"So resurrecting that black hole I was in is good for both of us?" He shook his head and headed for the motorcycle.

"I think it is," I answered, climbing on behind him. "We can make a night of it with candles and wine," I whispered in his ear.

Jerry made a grunting sound and started the bike.

When he dropped me off in front of Tarot and Tea, I asked, "What are you going to do with the rest of the day?"

He made a face. "I'm going to get Sam to use the database to look into this Lucille person, and call the ME. Does that meet with your approval?"

"Jerry, come on. I know you didn't like the session, but I thought it was helpful. I only asked because I worry when you're at loose ends."

"Afraid I'll do something stupid?"

"No. I'm afraid you'll get into a funk."

He made a face. "Don't worry about that—I have anti-depressants."

He revved the bike and took off, leaning into the impossible angle he took around the corner. Jerry was in a dangerous mood. I wondered if I should go see Cynthia on my own—maybe she could give me some pointers on how to deal with him when he was like this.

I opened the door to Tarot and Tea and picked up the cat waiting for me. I hugged her close, feeling her fur tickle my nose. I would have loved to spend the day with Jerry but I couldn't put my own life on hold because he'd been laid off— I had bills to pay and little money to pay them. Hopefully he wouldn't have a motorcycle accident and end up in the hospital. "Come on, Tabby—let's get you some breakfast." I put her down and she followed me back to the kitchen area, her plaintive meows making me laugh. She was fat from the winter, her fur thick and luxurious, but she acted as though she was starving.

I was rearranging books on the shelves when I heard a whispery voice next to me. "What has happened to that poor woman?"

I jumped and turned, seeing Mrs. Browning's concerned rheumy eyes trained on mine. "If you mean Sarah, she's still in jail."

"That is utterly ludicrous. There's more to this case than meets the eye and no one seems to be heading in the right direction."

"What do you mean?" I asked, but she'd already turned away and was perusing the new books I'd just gotten in, her back to me.

I decided not to call Jerry to give me a lift home. It was nice out for a change, the sun casting cloud shadows all along the sidewalk. I could hear birdsong and saw several birds with bits of stick and other nest-making materials in their beaks as I walked along. But when several men hurried past me I grew nervous. They were dressed in camouflage, guns strapped to their hips. Why wasn't the chief arresting these people? Was she waiting for another incident to happen? Because with the mood in town I could see some poor sap shot to death for taking a walk in the woods for no reason other than being in the wrong place at the wrong time.

Jerry's bike was parked in the alley when I reached my house, and when I opened the door he was sprawled on the loveseat reading a magazine, a beer on the table next to him. He looked up when I came in and swung his legs to the floor. "I found out some interesting news today," he said. "The ME says there's a set of prints on that gun that matches someone in the database. Unfortunately the guy's dead."

"Why were his prints in there?"

"He was in the army. But listen to this—his army duty was during WWII."

"What about the newspaper clippings?"

Jerry shook his head. "Nothing on those, but the jacket had DNA—Ray's checking on it, but it's very old."

"Does he have a name on the prints?"

"Yeah. They belonged to Grant Cumberland's son, Timothy, Sarah's father."

"But—"

"I know. He died in the war far from here."

"That was his Colt, wasn't it?"

"Apparently so. Not sure how it got from wherever he died to the woods behind Ames."

"What about Lucille? Did you look her up today?"

Jerry nodded and grabbed his beer, taking a long pull. He wiped foam off his lip before saying, "According to Sam, who dipped into the FBI database, she's living in Providence in an old age home. I wrote the address down. If you're interested I'd be willing to take a trip up there."

"Seems like she's our only real clue. I can't imagine a ghost using that Thompson machine gun to shoot up the school."

Jerry made a derisive sound. "Not likely. Apparently

Lucille's the last relative. But I'll tell you, Summer, if she's deceased or we find her and she has nothing of interest to tell us, we're SOL. Sarah is going to need a very good lawyer."

I went into the kitchen and pulled out salad makings, a frozen bag of chicken and some leftover brown rice. "You were very productive today," I said, grabbing out the wine bottle and pouring myself a glass. "I'm impressed."

Jerry moved up behind me and put his arms around my waist. "I'm as interested in getting her off as you are. And now that I'm not working I have time to look into things."

I turned. "Are you saying you might be enjoying this lay-off?"

Jerry smiled a little smile. "When I'm on the payroll I have to follow protocol."

"Lucky you have a good friend who's willing to put his career on the line."

"Sam? He won't do anything to jeopardize his career. What he checked into today was stuff the chief told him to do. And as long as he was in there—"

"He decided to look up one more name?"

Jerry grinned. "When can we go to Providence?"

I began to make dinner, thinking about my store and the wedding plans I had to follow up on. "How about Sunday? The store's closed and traffic shouldn't be bad. I don't want to ask Agnes to take over again—especially this close to her big day."

Jerry nodded. "In the meantime I'll see what else I can get from Ray. Maybe he managed to pull some other prints or DNA off that jacket. I still can't believe all those prints belong to a man who's been dead for over seventy years."

18

I took off early from Tarot and Tea the following day to catch up with last minute wedding preparations. The date was looming and I hadn't been thinking about it with the case and my relationship with Jerry. On the phone I arranged for Flowers and Frills to deliver the flowers to the Victorian home for the elderly where the wedding would take place, hoping Mabel, the owner, could hear me clearly. She was somewhat deaf and sometimes pretended she could hear when she couldn't. The orders that people got were not always what they expected, carnations turning into nasturtiums and larkspur turning into foxgloves. The only thing I was sure of was Agnes's bouquet of yellow sweetheart roses and sprigs of hyacinth.

Agnes had worked for Mabel before Agnes inherited money, and Mabel thought of her as a daughter. Mabel had been added to the guest list which was growing longer and longer as the days went on. Agnes was becoming more and more frantic as the day approached and I could tell she wasn't sleeping well despite the calming herbs the holistic doctor had prescribed.

When my phone rang I answered it, expecting another frantic call from my best friend. I wasn't disappointed. "My dress is too tight now!" she wailed. "I can't wear it!"

"Come and get me and I'll take a look," I said. "But you have to give me a ride home after. Jerry is expecting me to fix dinner tonight."

"I'll be there in ten minutes."

Once we reached her house Agnes led the way into her bedroom and walk-in closet. When she undressed she looked as she always had—slim hips, small breasts and a stomach flatter than most of the women who weren't pregnant.

She pulled the dress off the hanger and slipped it on. "See?" she said, pointing at her stomach.

"See what? The dress fits a little better now, if that's what you're referring to. Last time you tried it on it was too loose."

She made a moue and pulled it off over her head. "You're just saying that—everyone will know, Summer, and I haven't even met Sam's parents yet. They're going to think I'm a floozy. And what if I balloon out in the next two weeks?"

I laughed. "You do not look like a floozy, and no one can tell you're pregnant. And I highly doubt you'll balloon out in the next two weeks. Stop worrying and enjoy it. This is hopefully the one and only time you'll get married. Try and have fun."

"That's exactly what Sam keeps saying. He's like a little kid in a candy store right now. I've never seen him so excited."

"Take a clue, Agnes. It's going to be a super day— the weather should be warm and sunny. All the preparations are coming along fine. Enjoy yourself—it's your big day!" I gave her a hug.

"How are you and Jerry?" she asked, putting her dress carefully back on the hanger.

"He's anxious to talk with the missing sister, Lucille Cumberland. We're going to Providence on Sunday. I really hope we can find some evidence to clear Sarah. The longer this goes on the worse it is for her, especially since the parents are convinced of her guilt. Did you know there are witch-hunts going on? Ames has turned into Salem, Massachusetts."

"I haven't been out much, but when I was at the market the other day it seemed like even the people I know avoided looking at me. I had on a sleeveless shirt and I wondered if it was about my tattoos, but I've never had reactions like that before."

Agnes led the way toward the kitchen and I followed her, admiring her immaculate stainless steel appliances, and the simple bamboo cabinets with the metal pulls that looked like twigs. Her counters were black marble, polished to a high shine. I wondered if she had a housekeeper, because if not, she obviously spent a lot of time cleaning.

Agnes pulled two cans of orange soda out of the refrigerator and handed me one. "Sam says the chief refuses to look into other possibilities."

"I know and I don't understand why."

I was at Tarot and Tea the next morning when Agnes called my cell phone.

"Sam said that Jerry just called and asked him to go with him out to the woods again."

Jerry and I had had coffee together early and he had said nothing about this. "Is Sam going to do it?"

"You know Sam, he can't say no to Jerry. I think they might be on their way now."

I glanced at the clock on the wall—eleven-thirty.

"What should I do?"

"There's nothing you can do. I'm not that worried about Sam, although his arm is still in a sling. He'll be careful, but Jerry is already on thin ice. Sam said he's fixated on this case and insists that the chief will reinstate him if he solves it."

"That isn't true and the more I think about her the more I think she's purposely ignoring evidence."

"There will have to be a trial. Maybe Sarah will get off because it's so circumstantial."

"The gun has Sarah's prints on it and it was at her house. The chief will get huge kudos for solving this case. I've had the feeling all along that something was up with her, but I still don't know what."

"Sam said he doesn't completely trust her—says she has some skeletons in her closet. If she doesn't solve this case she could be in trouble with the DA."

"Really? That makes sense considering her dismissive attitude about the sister and those drug pushers she never wanted to pursue. Unfortunately she's in charge of Jerry's career, and if he gets caught doing this she could fire him."

"I hope they come back soon. I do not want to go through another night of worry."

"I don't either." I looked up as Douglas walked toward me with a serious expression on his face. "Got to go," I told her, pressing end on my phone.

"Agnes is involved in this mess?" he asked.

"No, her cop husband-to-be is, though. He and Jerry are heading out to the woods to try and find more evidence. We've already been, but he thinks we may have missed something,"

"They won't find anything—at least not yet. I think your line of inquiry will give you better results."

"My line of—how do you know about that?"

Douglas didn't smile. "Right now there is a killer loose and I'm telling you that Jerry and Sam will not find him out there."

"So where is he then?"

"Follow up on what you planned to do and things will fall into place."

I turned to take money from another customer. When I looked around for Douglas to ask him a question, he wasn't there. I searched through the store but he'd disappeared as neatly as he always did. I wondered if any of my other customers noticed his unusual ways of coming and going.

I headed into the shelves to straighten up the books wondering why he couldn't just tell me what he obviously knew. Was there some list of rules posted somewhere to tell ghosts what they could and could not do? I saw the blackboard in my mind: Number one rule—Ghosts may not reveal any knowledge they are privy to, either past, present or future. If they fail to follow this simple rule they will—what—be banned from ghost hood? Sent back to the bardo for all eternity? Be shunned by all the other self-respecting ghosts? I laughed at the absurdity of it all and headed back to the counter to help another customer.

The one good thing about what Douglas told me was that Jerry and Sam would not find the crazy man, despite the evidence we'd come across on our earlier trip. I could stop worrying about another shooting and the possibility of Jerry being wounded or worse, but I also knew that when he got back from this wild goose chase he'd be furious and even more frustrated. I would have another night of trying to settle him down. It was similar to trying to calm a caged animal—Jerry was spring loaded in the pissed off position, and if something good didn't happen for him soon he would blow.

As I suspected Jerry arrived home late after drinking several beers with Sam at the Pig and Pint. He was in a black mood and even though I tried to cheer him up he refused to snap out of it. "I'm glad you didn't find anything," I said. "I was worried that the guy was hiding out there somewhere. I was afraid you'd get shot."

He dropped onto the loveseat, his shoulders hunched. "I'd rather get shot than sit around like an f-ing bump on a log."

"Jerry, what if I go talk to the DA? She sounds like a reasonable person and maybe I can find out the truth of what's going on."

Jerry looked up, his eyes bloodshot. "Myra Proctor is a hard-ass, Summer. She isn't going to agree with your assessment of Sarah, especially with all the evidence her golden girl collected."

"Sandra Marshall is her golden girl?"

"Myra's the one who hired her after my crooked dad got booted off the force."

I ignored the crack about his dad, knowing that it still pained him to realize his father was on the take. "I'm still going to try. Sam doesn't trust Sandra Marshall and I don't either. Something fishy is going on."

While I cleaned up the kitchen after dinner Jerry drank two more beers, adding a scotch chaser. I saw his heavy-lidded gaze watching me and knew exactly what was coming next. When he got off the couch and moved unsteadily toward me I put up my hand. "No. You're drunk and we are not having sex."

"Come on, Summer," he whined.

"You need to get yourself together. If you can't stop behaving like this I want you to move back to your house. And why isn't Cynthia helping you? Are you seeing her?"

Jerry stared at the floor. "I've been seeing her for months. I'm tired of it."

"And what did she say the last time you went?"

"She told me to stop feeling sorry for myself and do what the chief told me to do."

"And you haven't been back? I thought that was part of your agreement to get reinstated."

"Goddamn it, Summer—get off my case!"

Jerry slept in the guest room after a shouting argument that I was sure my nosy neighbor could hear.

I only had two more days to get through before our trip to Providence but

I had the strangest sense that Jerry was going to lose it. When Agnes called to tell me that Sam had spilled the beans to the chief about their recent trip to the woods a nervous twitch went through my stomach.

"Sam didn't mean to tell her," Agnes assured me over the phone. "It came up in a way that he wasn't expecting and he just blurted it out."

"Why did Sam agree to go out there again?"

"You know how Sam feels about Jerry—the guy walks on water. They found something else, did Jerry tell you?"

"No. Jerry was in a foul mood and we had a huge argument. He left before I got up this morning. What was it?"

"Some ripped out pages of that journal. Sam took it into the police station and handed it over to the chief."

"What did it say?"

"Something about payback time and they would never forget him after this."

"He sounds like the shooter, Agnes. I wish they'd let Sarah out."

"Sam said she might be taken to the hospital for observation. I guess she refuses to eat."

"Oh my god. That's terrible! And I haven't been to see her at all."

I hung up and got ready to close up the store, my thoughts scattering like autumn leaves in a high wind. Why hadn't Jerry mentioned this new evidence? He had an appointment with Cynthia tomorrow and hadn't yet mentioned whether he wanted me along. Would she ask him about his homework?

I was in the kitchen when Jerry came in, a few leaves blowing in with him. I turned to look at him but he was taking his jacket off, a scowl on his face.

"I heard what you found yesterday," I said.

He stared at me. "What are you talking about?"

"The woods? Sam? At this rate you'll be fired before your month-long trial is up."

He stared at me with his eyes narrowed. "I had to take another look with a detective who knows his way around."

"Instead of me, the one who found all the newspaper clippings? What did the chief say about the journal pages?"

"Agnes knew about the pages from the journal?"

"Yes. Unlike you, her man shares everything with her." I turned back to what I was doing, feeling my face turn hot.

"You're in a piss poor mood," he said, coming into the kitchen. He pulled open the fridge and took out a beer.

"What was the consensus about what the journal entry meant?"

"Sam agrees with me that the shooter wrote it. But the chief says it's not enough. Apparently we need a signed confession before she'll let Sarah off the hook."

"Did you see the chief?"

Jerry scoffed. "Hell no. Sam called me after he talked to her."

"Jerry, I'm really annoyed with you right now. You're keeping things from me and you haven't talked to me about your four months of hell. Did you forget you have an appointment with Cynthia tomorrow morning?"

Jerry made a little harrumph sound and shook his head. "Remember what you told me you didn't like about Tom?"

"That he mothered me?"

Jerry nodded. "Yeah, that. See any similarities here?"

"No. Cynthia asked us to be honest with one another—that is not the same as mothering."

"Maybe I should head home until this case is done. I really can't listen to your bullshit right now."

"So apparently our relationship is less important to you than running around half-cocked with your buddy Sam. I have half a mind to go and talk to Cynthia on my own."

"Do it—what do I care? Get her on your side and then the two of you can gang up on me."

"That's not fair!"

"What isn't fair is you telling me how to conduct myself. I'm a cop and I've been one for a long time.

What do you want from me?"

I opened the fridge and pulled the bottle of wine out. I poured a glass and turned to him. "I want to know how you felt during those four months. I want you to share what's on your mind and what your plans are. I hate finding out after the fact."

"What I want is not to hear about what a bad boy I am for doing something with my former partner." He finished his beer and threw the bottle into the garbage can.

"That's recycles," I said.

Jerry pulled it out and threw it violently into the other can. "Satisfied? I'm going out for a while. If I don't come back tonight don't call the police. I'm a big boy and can take care of myself."

He slammed out the front door and I heard his motorcycle growl to life. A second later it roared away.

"Agnes, Jerry is really on the edge of losing it," I told my friend on the phone after I'd gotten my tears under control. "He just took off and I think he's planning to get drunk. I'm pretty sure I won't see him again tonight."

"Sam says this suspension is bringing up bad memories. It's like he's slipping into that place again."

"Cynthia asked him to tell me about his breakdown, but of course he hasn't said a damn word about it. He's so closed up right now. I don't know what to do."

"Sam says when Jerry gets this way the best thing to do is leave him alone. He has to work things out for himself."

"Hard for me to do."

Agnes laughed. "Don't I know it? If you want to

come over I've got a stew on the stove."

"No thanks, Agnes. My face is red and swollen from crying and I'm already in my pj's."

"I'll call tomorrow," Agnes promised before she hung up.

19

Jerry came home at three in the morning, his drunken arrival pulling me out of a dream. I had been in the past with Grant Cumberland, my part in his life unclear. I rubbed the sleep out of my eyes as Jerry stumbled into the bedroom and fell face down on the bed.

"Jerry?"

"Wha…"

"Don't you want to get undressed?"

But Jerry was already fast asleep, his snores giving him away. He smelled like a brewery and after taking off his shoes and covering him with a blanket I went into the guest room to spend the rest of the night. Cutty followed me, as though he didn't want to be anywhere near the snoring smelly replica of the human he had always liked. I lay awake until I heard the birds singing and then fell into a stuperous sleep only to be awakened by my cell phone ringing in the kitchen. I staggered from the bedroom and hurried to answer it, hoping that Jerry would sleep through the insistent noise. I did not want to see or speak with him until I'd sorted through my feelings.

It was Cynthia on the line. "Summer, is Jerry with you?"

I looked at the clock, shocked to see it was nearly nine. Should I be honest with her or make up some story about why Jerry had missed his appointment? I decided to go with the truth. "He's here but he got home drunk at three in the morning and passed out. He's still asleep."

There was silence for a moment and then she said, "I need to speak with one of you. I've come to a conclusion about Jerry's situation and why he's reacting so badly to his suspension. Could you come by for just a few minutes? I'll set some time aside for Jerry late this afternoon if you think you can get him here."

"I can certainly try, although we had a huge fight last night and he may not be speaking to me."

"And yet he came home to you instead of going to his own house."

"True, and I didn't expect it. As far as coming in, yes I'd be willing if you think it could help. I'm already late for work."

After I hung up I snuck into my room and dressed. When I closed the door behind me he was still sound asleep, his snores regular and deep.

The cabbie dropped me off in front of Cynthia's office fifteen minutes later. "Can you wait for me? I need you to take me to Tarot and Tea."

"Sure thing, lady. It's your dime."

I knew I'd be racking up the bill but my choices were limited until I had a chance to buy a car. It seemed as though everything was conspiring to keep me from doing so.

Five minutes later I was sitting in front of Cynthia, my hands folded in front of me.

"Thank you for coming, Summer. This has been very hard for you, I know. I was up until the wee hours myself last night."

She did look exhausted, I noticed, with deep circles under her lovely eyes, her clothing and make-up not as perfect as I'd remembered.

"I have already spoken with the chief about my thoughts and I hope she will take them into consideration, especially since I hold her responsible for what has happened to Jerry."

"What—?"

Cynthia held up her hand. "Please let me finish before you ask any questions." She took a sip of water and sighed before turning to me again. "I have been seeing Jerry for nearly a year now and I've tracked his progress carefully and documented it in my notes. He was doing very well and we had talked about terminating his therapy—that was when I asked him to speak with you to resolve your issues. It had become patently obvious that he was not over you, and had not delved into his feelings. In the meantime the chief had him go undercover, something I did not approve of. But you know Jerry, he was anxious to please her, and as you are well aware, he's very good at what he does."

Cynthia paused again, her gaze going to the window where blowing bits of catkins floated by, caught in the wind that had suddenly arisen. She turned back to me. "I think the undercover job, coupled with this latest shooting brought up the demons Jerry left behind from your last case. And the drugs he felt he had to take to seem believable further exacerbated it. When he took matters into his own hands and brought Cable in he pushed the chief into an untenable place. Did you know the town council is considering replacing her?"

I shook my head no.

Cynthia nodded and continued. "When the chief suspended him after all the good work he'd done, Jerry fell into a dark place. I have to say it was very poor timing on Sandra Marshall's part and I wonder about her motivations."

"Motivations? You think she—?"

Cynthia nodded, her eyes turning dark. "Yes, I do. I think Sandra Marshall has lost her moral compass. If she does not heed what I've told her about Jerry I will go to Myra Proctor. I'm hired by the department to help with psychological issues that arise due to job-related stress and so on. This is a clear example of such and I think the chief knew what she was doing."

"Did you know about her nephew?"

"What nephew?"

"Sandra Marshall's nephew was part of the meth gang, and from what I've heard, the chief warned them about a possible raid before Jerry and Sam went out there. And she whisked her nephew out and put him into re-hab."

Cynthia's eyes went wide. "I'll give her the benefit of a doubt, but if she does not respond to my request to reinstate Jerry, I will go straight to Myra." Cynthia stood and went to her desk. "I have some papers here that I want you to take to Jerry. One of them is a copy of the letter I wrote to the chief and also a few of my notes. And as I mentioned on the phone, I've set aside a slot at four-thirty if he can make it."

I left a few minutes later after thanking her profusely for caring enough to look into all of it. I was shocked when this formal and circumspect woman pulled me into a hug.

Instead of having the cab drop me off at Tarot and Tea I had him take me home. I had to give Jerry the good news. But when I reached my house Jerry's motorcycle was gone.

I walked to Tarot and Tea, not surprised that a few of my customers were milling around looking annoyed.

"Sorry," I said sliding the key in the lock. "I was called in for police business this morning."

I opened the register, my thoughts going back to what Cynthia had told me. And then I thought about Jerry. Where could he have gone? He was not in a good place and I worried about what he might be up to.

My cell phone rang an hour later. Jerry. I slid my finger across the screen. "Jerry? Where are you?"

"I'm having coffee with Sam and a bit of the hair of the dog. Where did you go this morning?"

"Cynthia asked me to come in—she—"

"Cynthia? Why?"

"I'm trying to tell you. She gave me a copy of a letter she wrote to the chief. Can you come by Tarot and Tea? I think you'll want to see this."

Jerry walked into the store fifteen minutes later looking tired and rumpled, his thick hair sticking up in tufts. After my meeting with Cynthia I felt an immediate need to give him a hug, my arms wrapping around him for a long moment.

"I guess you're not still mad?" he whispered.

I shook my head and pulled away. I reached into my bag and handed him the letter. "Take a look at this," I said.

While Jerry read I looked over his shoulder.

Dear Ms. Marshall,
At your request, Detective Jerry Brady has been in therapy for nearly a year. I have watched him go from a disturbed and unbalanced man into the strong and capable officer he was before the events of last summer. I had given him the green light to quit therapy just before he was assigned the undercover job. Despite the

psychological hardships and the drugs he became addicted to, he has since managed to overcome his addiction and has proven to me that his mental health is intact. But, this latest suspension you placed on him has sent him backward in a most disturbing way. I do not like to accuse you of wrongdoing, Sandra, since we have been friends and colleagues for some time, but I wonder about the wisdom of your decision. Jerry has told me that Sam was not punished in similar fashion. This fact is disturbing to me.

I hesitate to mention this, but I wonder if your job security is involved in any way? I know Jerry is on a career path toward chief but has been hindered by his father's checkered past. With this latest black mark on his record it would seem you wish to prevent him from moving up in the ranks. If you do not see fit to reinstate Detective Brady to full duty I will be forced to speak with the DA, Myra Proctor. Please do not make me take this step.

Sincerely,
Cynthia Blackwell, Ph.D.

Jerry looked shocked as his gaze met mine. "This is unexpected."

"She gave me some of her notes too," I said, handing him another sheaf of papers. "She told me she thought the chief had lost her moral compass."

"Wow."

"Can you go and see her at four-thirty? She's holding a spot open."

Jerry nodded slowly, his brows furrowing. "I feel like a little kid whose kind aunt is explaining his bad behavior to his parents."

"What bad behavior? What did you do to cause

Sandra Marshall to come down on you like that?"

"I don't know, but I figured I deserved it."

"Jerry, you've been through hell and come back, and now she's keeping you from the one thing you love."

Jerry smiled sadly and reached for me, drawing several looks from older customers. "My job is not the only thing I love, Summer."

I met his soulful gaze. This Jerry was not the Jerry of yesterday. "I agree with Cynthia—I think Sandra's worried about her job."

Jerry frowned. "I'm not in any position to take her job away. For one thing there are several steps I'd need to take."

"Whatever her reasons for suspending you, they're wrong. And I also believe she's ready to send an innocent woman to jail. Will you help me prove it?"

Jerry looked around for the first time, his gaze coming to rest on Mrs. Browning who I suspected had been eavesdropping. He turned back to me, his brown eyes soft. "Tomorrow is Sunday and I've already printed out directions to Lucille's apartment. Sam agrees that's she's important to the investigation. He also told me to give you this." Jerry reached into his leather jacket and pulled out the journal pages that had been ripped out of the journal. "He thinks you might get some psychic hit off it."

I took the stiff paper. "I don't know what else I could come up with."

"Just look at it, would you? Maybe we missed something." He glanced at his watch. "If I'm going to get to Cynthia's office by four-thirty I better get a move on."

He hurried toward the door and opened it before turning back. "See you at home?"

I nodded and smiled, his use of 'home' causing a

warm feeling to move through my body. He always called it 'your house', not home.

Once I reached my cottage I took another careful look at the pages. *The die is cast now—there is no going back. I hope this will finally stop my pain.* It was after I read those words that my hands began to tingle and I had the vision.

A man with brown hair searched through the rubble of a bombed out building, his hands cut and bleeding as he tried to free a man who was trapped under a large piece of foundation material. Another man wearing a uniform lay flat on the ground, but this one was older and very obviously dead. I could see how similar his features were to the other. Another scene superimposed itself over this one and I saw a different man shouldering the gun. His features had the same configuration as the other men, all of them square-jawed with deeply set eyes and heavy brows. I tried to see where he was, but the background was faded and indistinct like a photograph in which the subject was the only thing in focus. It was only when I saw him raise the gun and begin to fire that I realized what I was witnessing. But before he could mow everyone down another figure superimposed itself over his and the gunshots went wild. I saw the two teachers and the five children go down, the chaos and blood overwhelming me. And then I was sliding into unconsciousness, happy to be relieved of sight.

"Summer, Summer!"

I opened my eyes staring up into Jerry's very concerned brown ones.

"What happened to you?" he asked, pulling me up to sitting.

"I guess I fainted." I tried to laugh but the memory of

what I'd seen came drifting back making me almost physically ill. My hand flew to my mouth and I moaned, causing Jerry even more worry.

"What is it?"

"I saw him—I saw the man who killed those children. It was so awful. But Jerry, something kept him from killing everyone in that building—it was a ghost who stopped him." And then I was crying and holding on to Jerry as though he was a life buoy in a turbulent sea.

20

"**S**ummer, you saw the shooter. Can you describe him?"

I nodded, wiping ineffectually at my tear-stained cheeks. I was sitting on the couch now, Jerry next to me. "He looked like the newspaper clippings I've seen of Grant Cumberland—same deep-set eyes, same square face shape."

"We need to get you with a police sketch artist. This is the break we've been waiting for."

"Except that I didn't really see him, Jerry. I had a vision. And what about the ghost?"

But Jerry would not be deterred, his bright gaze never leaving my face. "We know it can't be Grant. Is there any chance Grant's son, Timothy, wasn't killed in the war?"

"I saw his obituary when I was searching for Grant's. So I don't think so."

"Mistakes can be made. Maybe—"

"The shooter was too young to be Grant's son."

"Grant's grand-son? I didn't think he had one."

"You're right—there is no mention anywhere that Timothy had a son and Sarah never mentioned a brother."

Jerry stared into space. "Maybe we'll discover something when we talk to Lucille tomorrow."

I'd forgotten all about the trip we'd planned. The week had been crazy and full of surprises. "What happened with your appointment with Cynthia?"

Jerry smiled, his gaze settling on mine. "She is determined to get me reinstated, said she'd talk to Myra if the chief didn't come through. But of course you knew that from the letter. I read her notes and they were very interesting. She seemed to think that my breakdown went back to my father's suicide—that I'd stuffed it and didn't deal. When we got involved in Yvonne's murder and you were nearly killed, it broke through whatever barriers I'd put in place. It's why I lost it so badly."

I reached out and took his hand, twining my fingers through his. "Smart lady. I like that she's got your back."

"Should I make something to eat? You still look a bit green around the edges."

"I'd love that," I said, settling against the cushions. When Cutty jumped on the couch and licked my face I realized he hadn't been fed. "And would you mind—?"

Jerry rose from the loveseat. "Come on, little buddy," he said, heading into the kitchen. Cutty jumped off and trotted after him.

Jerry made omelets with cheese and spinach and brought our plates into the living room. We ate sitting on the loveseat without much conversation, and when we'd finished Jerry cleaned up. A half hour later he picked me up and carried me into the bedroom before proceeding to undress me. "Jerry, I—"

"Don't worry. I'm not doing this to ravish you. I just want to make up for my asinine behavior. You need a good night's rest before we head up to Providence." He paused in his systematic work and stared at me. "Would you rather I slept in the guest room?"

"No," I said emphatically. "I want your solid body next to me tonight."

He smiled and continued what he'd begun, and when he climbed in beside me and pulled me against him I drifted into a dreamless sleep.

I woke to the smell of espresso, a warm feeling stealing through my well-rested body. Jerry was really here, and barring any unforeseen events, we would talk with Lucille later today. My handsome detective boyfriend was about to get reinstated, and with any luck we might get Sarah off after all. The past month's frenetic activities were finally coming to an end. I stretched and rolled out of bed and padded into the kitchen.

"Good morning," Jerry said in a tone I had not heard in months. He was wearing his faded green T-shirt, loose sweats hanging on his narrow hips, his hair appealingly mussed. "Are you ready for our big day?"

I took the cup he held out, pulling my gaze from him to the window. "Clear weather? Amazing."

Jerry smiled, his eyes bright. "I let Cutty out and I don't know where Mischief got to—that cat meowed pathetically until I opened a can of tuna."

I laughed. "He's unrelenting when it comes to food."

"I'd like to get an early start," Jerry said, taking a sip of his cappuccino. "I hope to hell that woman is still alive—by my calculations she has to be in her eighties."

"If she came up on the database there's a good chance she is."

Jerry nodded. "I fixed French toast." He handed me a plate. "I'm going to take a shower."

I watched him leave the kitchen wishing we had time to roll around in bed for a while. With all our recent arguments it had been too many days. I ate the French toast, put the dishes in the dishwasher and went to dress.

When we left a half hour later I felt like the Michelin man. It was in the low fifties outside and I'd added a warm sweater, long underwear, heavy socks and boots, and a down jacket. I grabbed my helmet from the closet and slid it on over my hair. He gave me the directions but Jerry did not have a system set up for us to talk to each other. The best I could do was read them and yell in his ear.

It was nine when we drove out of Ames, headed northeast toward Hartford. The wind was icy and I pressed against his back trying to keep from shivering. Jerry seemed unaffected, his obvious good spirits keeping him warm. When we reached Hartford forty minutes later I checked the directions. "Route 384!" I yelled, pointing to a sign. "What's next?" he called.

"Route six!" I yelled back.

Once we reached route six we followed it all the way into Providence. I hung on to him for dear life as he roared around corners, leaning into the curves. I trusted him and had learned to lean with him instead of leaning the wrong way and unbalancing the bike, but it still got my adrenaline going. Once we reached the city we navigated the streets, me yelling in Jerry's ear until he finally pulled to the curb.

Jerry grabbed the printout out of my hands. "You sent us down the wrong street," he said accusingly, pointing.

"Sorry. I read the sign wrong. We aren't that far away," I added, looking up at the street sign ahead of us. "That's Winter Street," I said pointing. "We need to go right."

Jerry stuffed the directions into his jacket pocket. "Are you set?" he asked over his shoulder.

"I'm set."

He took off, barreled through the yellow light at the intersection, and making a tight right turn onto Adams, a narrow street full of old brick apartment buildings. As we parked the bike in front of number 8792, and took off our helmets, I noticed a few skinny cats wandering around, some plastic trash that seemed to have blown out of a trash bin, and weeds growing through the cracks in the uneven sidewalk. Wind blew between the buildings, lifting my hair and tangling it. The sun had been out on the trip up, but now clouds rolled in to obscure it, creating an ominous feeling exacerbated by the general decay.

We left the bike in a designated parking place that cost us four dollars in quarters, and carried our helmets with us across the street.

I followed Jerry into the shabby lobby, my nose wrinkling in distaste. It smelled like stale food, mold and some other medicinal scent I couldn't identify, all of them unsavory.

Jerry pulled out his badge, flashing it to the woman behind the counter while I stayed behind. I heard him ask for Lucille Cumberland and heard the woman's reply.

"Miss Cumberland has good days and bad days. She has dementia, you know."

"I didn't know," Jerry said in his cop voice. "We'll take our chances, if that's all right with you."

"Of course. Come with me. I'll show you where she lives."

We followed her up two flights of creaky stairs and down a long dark hall covered in a threadbare carpet. By the time we reached Lucille's room I was ready to be out of this claustrophobic place. Not only did it smell bad, there were also no hall lights and no windows to show the way. "Who pays for her?" I asked.

"She has a small trust that will likely run out before she dies. After that I hope to contact her family."

"Do you mean Sarah Cumberland, her niece?"

The woman looked confused. "No. The only family member I've been in touch with is Harry Dreiser, her nephew. He comes to see her once in a while."

Jerry and I exchanged a look just before she knocked on a door. "Lucille? You have company."

I didn't hear an answer but the manager opened the door and ushered us in. "Just come on down when you're through. I hope you get what you're looking for." She looked doubtful as she turned to walk away.

We entered the apartment and Jerry closed the door behind us. The hallway opened into a living room, a small kitchenette to our right, a bedroom on the left. In the living room ahead of us large casement windows that had not been cleaned in a while let in what light there was. The chairs and tables had seen better days, every surface covered with doilies and bric-a-brac that reminded me of stuff I'd turned up my nose at in second hand shops and yard sales. The rug was worn thin and stained and I felt sorry for this woman who had to live here.

She was sitting in a rocking chair facing the window, her iron gray hair the only thing we could see of her.

"Miss Cumberland?" Jerry moved toward her, motioning for me to stay where I was. He moved in front of her and stuck out his hand. "I'm Jerry Brady and this is," he motioned for me to come forward, "Summer McCloud. We were hoping to talk with you about your brother who died in the war and your niece, Sarah."

I stared down at the wizened woman in front of me, the vacant look in her eyes giving me a sinking feeling.

She seemed confused, her gaze darting between the two strangers who had invaded her space without her permission. "Who are you?" she asked in a cracked voice.

"I'm Jerry and this is Summer," Jerry said a second time, glancing at me.

"Hello, Miss Cumberland. We're so sorry to disturb you. Your niece Sarah is in jail for a crime she didn't commit and we thought perhaps you could help us with it."

"Call me Lucille, dear," she said, holding out her veined hand to me. I took it and sat on the stool at her feet.

"Sarah is a good girl but I haven't seen her since she was a baby. Her mother wanted nothing to do with me."

"Why is that?"

"I knew the secrets and Sarah's mother, Carol, couldn't abide it."

"The secrets?" Jerry asked, moving closer.

"Isn't that why you're here? To ask me about my brother's other family?"

"Your brother? Do you mean Timothy?"

She stared at me, her rheumy eyes losing some essence. A moment later she was humming, her mind far away.

I stood up and gazed at Jerry. "What now?" I whispered.

"Give her a minute."

It was only a couple of minutes later that Lucille came back to herself. "What was I saying? Oh yes, my brother's secret life. Carol never forgave him."

I knelt in front of her. "Your brother was killed in the war, isn't that right?"

"Yes, dear. He and my father both."

"So your brother had two families before the war?"

She nodded her thin dry lips turning up in a smile. "I told him he was being foolhardy, but he said he couldn't help himself. Molly was the loveliest girl, you see. And they had a child together, a boy. I always preferred Molly to Carol."

"Is this boy still alive?" Jerry asked.

"Oh, very much so. He comes to see me from time to time, but he hasn't been around for quite a while now."

"What is this man's name?" I asked, looking at Jerry.

But Lucille had fallen back inside herself and this time I had the feeling she wouldn't reappear, at least not in the next little while.

"Let's go," I said. "Maybe the woman downstairs has records of Lucille's visitors."

We left quietly and closed the door behind us and then stumbled down the pitch-black hallway to the stairs. When we reached the lobby the manager was again in back of the high desk, half-glasses perched on her thin nose.

"A man, you say?" she said, looking up. "Yes. She used to have a man who came by once in a while."

"How old would you say he was?"

"Perhaps in his sixties? It's so hard to tell these days. Nice looking with brown hair. He must have dyed it, but it did look quite natural."

"And his name?"

She leafed through the book where people signed in, going back many months. "John Smith it says here." She looked up. "Does that help?"

"Very much so," Jerry said. "Thanks for your time." He steered me out the door and toward the motorcycle. "He's the one."

"You think Lucille's nephew shot those kids and

teachers? Why would he?"

Jerry shook his head. "I have a gut feeling about it."

I chuckled. "That gut feeling is also called intuition—don't tell me you believe in that."

Jerry smirked at me. "Okay, Ms McCloud, what is your take on it all?"

"John Smith is the name of the guy Sarah dated, and if what Lucille said is true, he's Harry Dreiser, Sarah's half-brother. He had access to her house and she told me she showed him that gun. I think you may be right, but how in hell are we going to find him? He's definitely going by an alias. And also, what's his motive?"

"I don't know what his motive would be—maybe he's just crazy. Do you think this is the man you saw in your vision?"

"How do I know?"

"We need to get you and Sarah with a sketch artist and then send it through the database—maybe we'll get lucky."

"Why would he be in the database? I don't think he was in the army. And if he's using an alias we'll never find him."

"We can look into DMV records and if we don't find him, another trip to the woods?"

I met Jerry's gaze watching him wiggle his eyebrows. I laughed. "You think he's still there even though you've gone twice with Sam and once with me."

Jerry shrugged. "I suppose it makes more sense that he took off. Why would he shoot up the school and then stick around to be caught? But then again, why did you see a ghost out there who steered us to those newspaper clippings?"

Our eyes met. "The ghost wants us to find him. The man I saw in my vision looked almost exactly like that ghost."

"You said you saw two men in your vision?"

"I did. They looked very similar except one was dead and had gray hair and the other was brown-haired and alive."

"Timothy and Grant, I would imagine—father and son. Seems amazing they were together when the father died. I wonder when Timothy was killed."

"And the journal belonged to Timothy's son who no one knew existed—the second family. Those journal entries describe a man who seemed deranged. Did you mention them to Cynthia? Maybe she can shed some light on what his motivations might be." A drop of rain hit my head and when I looked up I saw a sky full of roiling clouds. "Maybe we should go have a coffee before we head back."

Jerry threw his leg over the bike. "Climb on. I saw a coffee shop on the way here."

Jerry and I sat in a booth at the Green Marble drinking coffee while we listened to the crash of thunder and watched rain pelt the glass, rattling the old panes. We talked about nothing in particular, both of us lost in thoughts about the case, and what would happen next. The storm passed by quickly, the sun peeking out again, wet leaves dazzling in the sudden brightness. We borrowed a towel and dried off the bike seats before heading toward home.

21

My optimistic attitude was knocked flat the next day when I got a call from the local fire department telling me that Tarot and Tea was on fire. By the time the taxi dropped me off the fire was nearly out, firemen pulling hoses around. I rushed through the open and smashed in door, frantically searching for my cat. "Ms McCloud," I heard a voice say as I coughed and choked on the acrid fumes, my heart in my throat. A hand came down on my shoulder, gently turning me around. "You can't be in here," the fireman said, a sympathetic expression in his gray-green eyes. "If you're looking for your cat, it ran out earlier and we have it in a cage in the truck."

"Thank you," I said, my eyes filling with tears. My store was destroyed, all the books ruined as well as my shelves and anything else made of wood. The only things that had survived were my crystal paperweights and a few metal goddesses and other icons. My glass showcase had been smashed to smithereens when a burned out beam fell down, all the jewelry burned beyond recognition.

I had checked on Tabby and was sitting on the curb when my cell phone rang. "I've been fired," Jerry said, his tone flat. "The chief told me she was shocked when she got the letter from Cynthia and was sure I'd put her up to it. I guess she thought it was my Italian charm," Jerry added, dryly.

"Jerry, someone torched my store."

"What? Are you okay?"

"I'm fine, just a little shaken. The firemen are still here."

"I'll be there in five minutes," he said, clicking off.

True to his word Jerry roared up five minutes later, his shocked expression going from me to my store and back again. "What the—"

"I should have expected it after the picketers."

"What picketers?"

"Didn't I tell you? There were a couple of people here a week or so ago with signs that I was a devil worshipper." I couldn't hold my tears back as I glanced again at my ruined store, all my merchandise gone.

Jerry sat next to me, his arm going round my shoulders. "Didn't we promise to not keep things from each other?" he asked gently.

"I forgot all about it. It was just another weird day in a sequence of weird days. Why did you get fired? Was this because of John Smith, aka, Harry Dreiser?"

"Yeah, partly. I have no business sticking my nose any further into this case, her words."

"So she didn't think the nephew we discovered was worthy of further discussion?"

"Not that she said. In her opinion we need look no further for the shooter."

"Her take on it from day one. Now what?"

"Now Cynthia talks with Myra, I suppose—not that I'm looking forward to that firefight. For all I know Myra will side with the chief."

"I highly doubt it, Jerry."

"I'm not feeling particularly optimistic right now,

especially looking at this mess. I may take us both down to the Pig and Pint."

I tried to smile. "Let Cynthia do her thing before you lose hope. The chief is the one who should be fired."

Jerry rose and headed to a fireman who had emerged from within the house. I heard him ask, "Do you know how the fire was started?"

I couldn't hear the response as the two men walked toward the fire truck. I stared into space, my mind numb. I had no idea if my insurance would cover the damage or how I was going to pay to replace all my merchandise. But the worst thing about it was that the fire was most certainly set by a person who lived in Ames.

I was silently crying when I felt Jerry's hand come into mine. He pulled me up. "I'm taking you down to the Pig and Pint and we're having some alcoholic beverages before we head home."

"What did he say? Does he know how it was started?"

Jerry nodded. "Someone left the gas burner on in back, made sure there were rags close to it and poured a bunch of paint thinner around. He asked me if you could have accidentally left that burner on and I said no, that you rarely even use it."

"I can't believe this. My cat could have been killed. How did the fire department find it?"

"Becky saw flames and called it in."

"Bless her witchy heart. If they hadn't gotten here, Tabby would be dead and there would be nothing left of this house."

"Leave them to finish up. They'll give you a full report tomorrow."

I pulled away from him and hurried over to the truck and pulled the cat carrier out. "I have to take him home.

Why don't you go to Pig and Point and I'll see you when you get back?"

Jerry frowned. "I'm not going anywhere without you."

Somehow Jerry found a way for me to hold the cat carrier in my lap while he drove us home on the bike. When we reached my cottage I hurried inside, not sure how to manage the meeting of Mischief and Tabby. They'd only had one encounter and it hadn't gone well. I put the carrier on the ground, and once Jerry was inside I closed the door. Before I could give Jerry instructions he opened the carrier and Tabby flew out.

I heard a growl from Tabby as he and Mischief, who had appeared as if by magic, faced off.

"Ignore them," Jerry said, heading to the kitchen. "They'll work it out better if we don't interfere."

I was still watching them when Jerry brought me a glass of wine, a beer in his other hand. He sat next to me. "I'm so sorry, Summer. Ted said it's definitely arson. What kind of insurance do you have?"

I closed my eyes and leaned back. "From what I could see all my papers burned up in the fire."

Jerry moved close, his thigh against mine. "We'll work it out. I'm sure you have some information we can look up—there are only two insurance companies in town you could have used."

I took a big sip and let out a long sigh. "It's good that we live in such a small town, but knowing that someone I might have met torched my store? Really creepy."

Jerry shook his head. "I wish you'd mentioned those picketers. I would have liked to question them and at least get their names."

"The chief sent a couple of cops by—maybe they wrote something down."

"You called the chief and not me?"

"Jerry, now is not the time to get huffy. I think you were off with Sam at the time."

A second later there was a loud crash as Cutty rushed in through the dog door, looking like a Tasmanian devil as he chased the two cats up on a table where they knocked over a vase.

"I think the cats have bonded in solidarity against the dog," Jerry commented, looking at me.

The next morning after Jerry took off for parts unknown, I had a taxi take me down to the used car lot. It was time for me to get my own wheels and stop expecting others to ferry me around. And besides, I had to pick up several things for the wedding and having a taxi do it just seemed wrong. I had the taxi driver take me past my store again, my tears starting as I surveyed the damage. I had to get on this sometime today, but not right now.

I spent the next hour looking at cars, trying to find one that would fit my budget and seemed intact engine-wise. The man who helped me seemed determined to find one for me and finally did. It was a dark blue Honda wagon that had seen better days, but the price was right. We spent another half hour setting up my billing and checking my credit. My payments would not be high. It wasn't long before I climbed behind the wheel and drove my purchase home.

Jerry's motorcycle was parked in the alley, and I wondered if I'd

find him drunk and passed out on my living room floor. He'd been very down the night before and he'd left before we had a chance to talk. I parked my new/old car next to his bike and walked to the front door. I was just about to put the key in the lock when it opened.

"Where have you been?" he asked, looking annoyed.

"I was buying a car."

I went to the kitchen to fill up Cutty's water dish, surprised that my dog wasn't there to greet me.

"A car?" Jerry asked, following me into the kitchen. "You should have waited for me. What did you get?"

"An old Honda junker. All I needed was something to get me around town. I'm tired of asking for favors."

"You got it at Mick's used car lot?"

"Yeah. Why?"

"He's a crook that's why. I hope he didn't cheat you."

"Where's Cutty?"

"Haven't seen him."

I looked in the bedroom and then checked out back but my dog wasn't there. The night before I'd shut him in the guest room for several hours after he chased Tabby and Mischief all over the house. Strangely enough Mischief and Tabby were tolerating each other and had both slept on the bed with Jerry and me. I opened the front door. "Cutty!" I called, cupping my hands around my mouth. I headed outside, scanning up and down the street. There was no sign of him.

When I turned Jerry was right behind me. "I didn't see him when I got back. Where could he have gone?"

I felt a rising panic. Had someone decided to escalate their attack on me by stealing my dog? "I don't know. Maybe he got out of the yard somehow."

A second later Jerry smiled and pointed down the street. I turned to see

Cutty hurtling toward us. I scooped him up. "What are you doing, Cutty? You know it's not safe out here." Jerry put his arm around my shoulders and steered me back inside and closed the door.

When I sat down Jerry sat next to me, his hands moving through Cutty's fur. "I want to work with you again—the two of us make a good team," he said out of the blue.

I stared at him. "Before or after we get you back on the police force?"

Jerry shook his head. "I'm not counting on anything, Summer. But if I'm not a cop anymore I'll have to do some kind of cop-type work. I can't stand not doing some form of this job."

"I have faith in Cynthia and Myra Proctor. Between the chief's nephew, what she did to you, and railroading an innocent woman, Sandra Marshall needs to be removed."

It was evening and Jerry and I had lit several candles and were sitting close together on the couch. We'd spent a couple of hours talking about the stress of the last couple of days and both of us were ready for a diversion. We were just about to kiss when my cell phone rang, the harsh chime startling us. I grabbed the phone off the coffee table and looked at the ID. "It's Agnes," I told him, answering.

"What are you up to?" her chipper voice asked.

"Jerry and I have some talking to do," I said, meeting Jerry's smoldering gaze. "I'll call you tomorrow, okay?"

By the time I hung up Jerry was unbuttoning my shirt, his fingers warm on my skin. "Is this okay?"

I nodded, unable to speak as his fingers traced patterns across my belly, his lips on my neck. When I let out a small gasp he looked up. "We haven't done this in a while—I don't want to push myself on you—especially after—"

"You aren't pushing yourself on me, " I managed to choke out as his hand slid up my thigh under my skirt. A few minutes later we were both on the rug on the floor, our hunger for each other taking away any sense of propriety. It was nearing nighttime and I hadn't closed the shades for the evening, but I couldn't interrupt what we were doing to close them now. Our clothes lay scattered across the floor, both of us naked when I heard a noise. Thinking it was a tree limb moving in the wind I returned my attention to where I straddled Jerry, his moans of pleasure egging me on. A second later the front door opened, revealing Sam.

"Oh shit!" he gasped, moving backward and closing it.

Jerry met my shocked gaze and gently pushed me off to find his jeans. "Don't go anywhere. I'll be right back."

I lay there trying to get my breathing under control as he walked shirtless to the door and went through, closing it behind him. I heard his voice and Sam's as I rose to find my clothing. I took it all with me and went into the bedroom where I turned on the lamp and climbed into bed. I felt embarrassed and humiliated as I buried my face in the pillow. Sam had just seen me naked and astride Jerry, riding him like the cowgirl of the century. I may as well have been yelling yippee ki yo ki yay and wearing a cowboy hat.

I heard Jerry come in, the sound of the door clicking shut behind him. "Summer? Where are you?"

"In here," I called.

Jerry appeared in the doorway. "Why are you hiding in here?"

"I'm embarrassed."

Jerry let out a laugh. "Sam's not a prude, Summer. He just got an eyeful, but who cares? Can we resume the position?" he asked, removing his jeans.

"I don't think I can now," I said in a small voice.

"Are you sure about that?" he asked, pulling off his jeans and moving in beside me. It didn't take long for me to forget all about Sam.

"So what did Sam want?" I asked some time later.

"He told me he overheard the chief talking on the phone with Myra Proctor. The chief was telling her all about me and how I'd gone against her over and over." Jerry smiled. "Sam apologized for barging in like that."

"Bet he regrets it," I giggled.

Jerry raised his eyebrows. "Actually I think it gave him some ideas. I guess his injury has been interfering with things."

"Did he say that?" I asked, incredulous.

Jerry chuckled. "No, not in so many words, but I know the guy. But getting back to why he came by, he thinks I should set up a meeting with Myra. He thinks this entire fiasco is because I've been nominated to be chief, and according to him, most of the force would be happy to see me in the position."

"When did that happen?"

"Two months ago? I didn't know anything about it. The city council can nominate whenever they see fit. I guess the chief found out and decided to take matters into her own hands."

"So all of this has been to protect her job?"

"That's what Sam thinks. It's hard for me to see the chief that way, but I do know she's ambitious as hell."

"And getting a conviction for the shooting would certainly help." I shook my head and pulled Jerry close. "I don't want to think about that right now."

He looked down on me, his mouth quirking. "Why

Ms McCloud, I do believe you're insatiable." He bent to kiss my collarbone, his tongue doing a magic dance across my overheated skin. And what followed was even more intense than the first time, mostly because of Sam's good news. Not only was Jerry beloved by the council, his fellow officers respected him as well. I let my own troubles drift away as I concentrated on Jerry. I won't comment on my methods, but let's just say I did my best to make him feel even more cherished.

22

Jerry and I were bleary-eyed and having coffee the following morning when Jerry's cell rang. He looked at the caller ID. "It's Cynthia," he said before sliding his finger across the screen. "You think that's a good idea?" he asked after saying hello and listening for a minute or two. "Sounds like that could lead to a nasty fight." He rubbed his hand across his stubbly chin. "Okay, if you say so. Summer too? All right."

"What?" I asked when he turned his bewildered gaze on me.

"She wants us to go and talk with Myra Proctor. Apparently she's already had a chat with her. I'm sure the chief is about to spit nails."

"When?"

"Sometime today, I guess. I'll call and set up an appointment. Now that you have a car we can avoid the rain."

I glanced toward the window where silvery rivulets ran down the squares of glass. Now that I thought about it I'd heard the rain start deep in the night, the wind making a whining sound in the cracks around my old windows. Storms seemed to be the norm whenever Jerry and I were intimate, the howling wind, branches snapping, rumble of thunder and bright flashes of lightning lending a wild element that increased our fervor. "Let's try for early. I have to call around to the insurance companies and find my policy."

"If she can't do early, would you be okay for this afternoon?"

I nodded and went to take a shower, hoping that the water would do a better job of waking me up. When I came out Jerry told me he'd made an appointment with Myra for five that afternoon.

"Good. That will give me time to check out all the damage and leave a note on my door. My customers are going to be devastated. What are you planning for the day?"

"I'm going to drop you off at Tarot and Tea and then check out your car. Is that okay by you?"

I smiled. "Sure, but don't go down to Mick's and start yelling if you find something you don't like—that's for me to do."

Jerry smirked. "Wouldn't dream of horning in on your fun."

He came in with me once we arrived at Tarot and Tea, his expression that of a cop. "This isn't as bad as it looks," he said. "Yeah, there's a lot of superficial damage, and your display case is ruined, but the fire didn't get into the walls because they're plaster, and I think all the wires are still intact." He kissed me goodbye and headed outside where I heard him grind the gears as he tried to put my car into second. I already had a proprietary feeling about my little car and hoped he would take it easy.

I spent the next couple of hours inventorying what had been ruined, keeping a tally sheet of everything I could remember. My computer was beyond repair, something I hadn't counted on. It would take me weeks to figure out what I'd sold, if I ever could. Around eleven I heard a quick knock and then Becky came inside. "Oh

Summer, how terrible!" she cried, looking around.

"I heard you were the one who called the fire department."

She nodded, her eyes filling. "I saw the smoke from down the street. I just happened to be at the bakery. I wish I'd seen who did this," she said, her eyes narrowing in anger.

"I think it was those picketers."

Becky nodded. "I saw them out there that day. What a bunch of cowards."

"Did you know them? Because I swear I've never seen them before."

Becky shook her head, moving to pick up some small items off the floor. "Does this belong to the store?"

I looked at the handkerchief with initials embroidered into one corner. "Definitely not."

She handed it to me. "Better give it to Jerry."

"Jerry's been fired."

Becky stared at me. "That cow. I never liked her."

"She may be on her way out. Jerry and I have an appointment with Myra Proctor, the DA, later today."

Becky took one more look around and headed toward the door. "All this is going to be fine," she said.

I started to ask whether this was coming from the witch part of her, or just an optimistic observation, but before I could say anything she was gone.

Jerry arrived at my store at ten minutes before five. I had changed from my loose peasant blouse and skirt into clothes I'd brought with me, but when Jerry's eyebrows shot up I wondered if I'd gone too far.

"You look really good, Ms McCloud," he said, admiring my crisp white blouse and black skirt, the fitted jacket I wore over it. "Very professional." He laughed.

"You think this will make her take you more seriously?"

"Better than my normal earthy attire."

"That's what you call bare feet and long skirts?"

I stared at him blankly. "How did my car do?"

"I'd give her a B-."

"Why not an A?"

"She's slow on the hills and doesn't corner as well as she should."

I shook my head. "I hate to think what you put my poor car through today."

After I wrote a note for my customers and thumbtacked it to the door I followed him out and climbed into the passenger seat, allowing him to continue to molest my girl. Jerry pushed down on the gas and the little car zoomed ahead. "Still running, isn't she?" he asked, smirking at me.

Myra was an attractive dark-haired woman in her late forties with wide gray eyes that seemed to take everything in. Her full lips were painted a color between red and brown, a hint of blush on her high cheekbones. She was dressed conservatively in a navy suit that fit her full curves, a cream camisole underneath. Despite her long painted nails and the spike heels she wore there was something implacable about her. She reminded me of teachers I'd had in grade school, ones who struck terror into my heart. She ushered us to two chairs in front of her desk and sat down behind it. "Cynthia seems to think there is some movement afoot to discredit you, Jerry. Is this true?"

Jerry looked over at me and then to Myra. "I didn't think so, but apparently I'm on some list for the chief's job."

Myra smiled but it didn't reach her eyes. "I've

known you for a long time, Jerry, and although you aren't a rule follower, I would never have picked you as a trouble-maker." She turned her gray eyes on me. "What is your take on all of this, Ms McCloud?"

"I think the chief feels that Jerry is a threat to her career and is railroading an innocent woman because she wants a quick conviction on her record."

"The woman arrested for the shooting?"

"That's just it—I'm certain she didn't do it."

Myra glanced at Jerry. "And what about all the evidence that points to her—what do you say about that?"

"The gun had other fingerprints on it and it was stolen from her house—it—"

"And it was returned. Don't you find that odd?"

"Not if the shooter wanted to blame it on her. And besides that, what is her motive?"

"A childless and loveless woman took her grief and anger out on a school full of kids."

I shook my head. "Sarah didn't do this and Sandra Marshall has refused to look into Sarah's aunt, who is the only living relative. I have to say I find it curious that Sarah was indicted to begin with. There's been a plethora of evidence pointing elsewhere but the chief has not pursued any of it."

"I don't know what this plethora of evidence is, but I trust Sandra Marshall's judgment."

"Do you? I heard the chief has some skeletons in her closet."

Myra's eyes widened. "You are quite outspoken, aren't you?"

"I don't want an innocent woman to go to jail and the chief seems bound and determined to put her there despite evidence that points to her innocence."

"Be careful—you're dangerously close to libel right

now." Myra turned to stare out the window, her long nails tapping on the desk. "Let's discuss Jerry now, shall we? That's the real reason Cynthia asked me to see you two."

"Jerry's dismissal seems intimately connected with the case," I said, looking over at him.

I could see the annoyance in her eyes as Myra turned to Jerry. "What is your take, Jerry?"

Jerry shrugged. "She kept me undercover for too long, and before my partner and I could bring the drug pushers in, she warned them off. Her nephew was part of the gang and I've heard that she somehow managed to grab him out of there and put him into rehab. That was before we caught Cable, which also pissed her off since I was on suspension at the time. And she fired yesterday because of the letter Cynthia wrote."

"Cynthia told me she felt that Sandra Marshall has been too harsh with you and felt obligated to bring this to my attention. She's sure the chief's behavior is due to fear of losing her job."

"By getting rid of the competition," I added.

Myra turned her gray eyes on me. "If this proves to be true, what would you have me do?"

"Jerry and I are fairly certain we know who did the shooting, but we need solid evidence. The chief refuses to entertain the possibility and if we don't act soon Sarah will go to jail for life."

"Isn't that a bit dramatic? She will be tried by a jury of her peers, Ms McCloud."

"If we can't look into this man, her half-brother, who Jerry and I both think is the shooter, she doesn't stand a chance. And she has a crappy lawyer."

"It sounds from what Sandra Marshall has told me that you and Jerry have been looking into quite a lot and without proper authority. Sandra has repeatedly warned

Jerry and now she's fired him due to his many offenses."

"But if we didn't do it, who would? And Sam's been helping Jerry. Ask him, he'll tell you. Can you find a better lawyer for Sarah?"

"You're asking the DA to find a good lawyer for someone who has been arrested for a crime?" Myra laughed. "Outspoken and cheeky. I'll recommend someone. Leave your number with my secretary. She should still be out there."

"So what are you going to do about the chief?" Jerry asked.

Myra looked down at her desk. "I suppose I will have to speak with the town council and find out if the rumors are true. And then I'll look into this person you mentioned. Do you at least have a name?"

"He goes by John Smith but we think his real name is Harry Dreiser," Jerry said. "Sam is checking with the DMV. We found his journal and some newspaper articles out in the woods that indicate some serious psychological problems, as well as the Colt semi-automatic pistol."

Myra nodded. "But are his fingerprints on the murder weapon?"

"We don't have his fingerprints and with my dismissal, no real way to get them," Jerry said, glancing at me.

Myra moved in her chair and stared out the large casement windows where some distant trees could be seen, their branches blowing wildly. When she turned back to us her expression had softened. "Based on what you two have told me and Cynthia's findings, I am giving you the authority to use whatever tools the police station has to offer to look for evidence on this person, Harry Dreiser. I will write a memo to that effect and send it over to the police station. In the meantime I will have a long conversation with Sandra Marshall and make a decision on the rest of it. If I find she's been abusing her authority there will be an investigation." She shook her head and sighed. "The position of chief in our small town seems to be fraught with problems. I'd hoped that Sandra's impeccable credentials would have brought the troubles of the past to a close." She stood to signal the meeting was over and Jerry and I rose from our chairs.

"Thank you both for coming in. If I need to see you again I'll let you know."

"Before we go," I said, reaching into my purse, "could you have someone check out this handkerchief? I found it in my store after it had been torched." I held it out.

Myra examined the embroidered square of linen. "Your store was set on fire?"

I nodded. "There were picketers there not too long ago and I have a feeling it was one of them or someone they know. It's related to this case and the furor that's taken over Ames about devil worshippers."

Myra stared at me. "I take it your store has something to do with the occult?"

"Tarot and Tea on the other end of town? Close to Bookers and Daily Bread."

Myra nodded. "Yes, I do recall it. I'll check out these initials and speak to the fire department. They'll corroborate that this was arson and not just an iron left on or some such thing."

"It was definitely arson," Jerry said, opening the door. "Thanks, Myra."

"Good to see you, Jerry," she said, smiling. They exchanged a look before Jerry ushered me out the door in front of him.

I left my number with the secretary as Myra had

suggested, hoping the name of a good lawyer would come soon, and then I followed Jerry out of the building toward where we'd parked the car.

"How do you think it went?" Jerry asked, actually opening the passenger door for me.

"I think it went well," I answered, sliding in. Once he was behind the wheel I turned to him. "Did you two have a thing?"

Jerry turned beet red. "Not really—I mean we—"

"You had sex?" I asked, horrified.

"It was a long time ago, before I met you. I was just a kid and so was she."

"No wonder she said something about you not following rules. Were you on the force at the time?"

Jerry sighed. "I was a new cadet and she was this hotshot assistant to the DA. It just happened."

"Emphasis on hot. She's really pretty."

"Summer, can we get back to what happened in there? Did you get the idea from what she said that I now have access to the database?"

"I think that's what she intimated. But give her a chance to send the memo first. I can't believe you and she—"

Jerry shook his head, his lips pressing together in irritation. "It was ten years ago, for god's sake!"

I smiled at his vehemence, imagining him as a young impressionable cadet. It was dark out now and the moon was already high above us. I suddenly wanted to be home in the comfort of my cozy cottage where I could forget about my ruined store, Sarah's problems, and Jerry's recent set of complications. "Let's go," I said, thinking about my dog impatiently waiting for his dinner. And it was time for ours too.

23

It was business as usual for the next few days, Jerry heading off to the police station and me talking with insurance adjustors and going through what needed to happen to get my store open again. Agnes met me there her eyes wide with shock when she saw all the damage.

"What are you going to do?"

"I'm going to get a contractor in here and fix it up, that's what."

"It looks almost impossible—and what about the smell? The smoke damage?"

"I hope they can rip out anything that absorbed smoke."

"I can't believe townspeople did this, Summer. It makes me want to move."

"It's crazy, I agree. Mob mentality—remember what happened after 9/11?" Agnes and I had been driving in the country when the planes hit the towers and when we stopped for gas a line stretched from the pumps down the road, people shrieking about Armageddon and filling up enormous barrels with gas. It was mass hysteria.

Agnes nodded. "I wonder about the wedding. It doesn't feel right to have it with Sarah still in jail and all this craziness going on."

"You are not postponing now. And I'm hoping we can get Sarah released before your day. I want her to be there for it."

"If she's still in jail I'm not going through with it."

"I told you that the DA is on it, right? Jerry and I are sure we found the guy. Now we just have to find him physically. He seems to have disappeared."

"Wouldn't you disappear after killing seven people? I'm surprised he didn't commit suicide after doing something like that."

"That's definitely a possibility. If he did I just hope we find his body and a suicide note confessing to the crime. Otherwise Sarah won't be released."

"I hate all of this. Once it's over I feel like moving into the country and never coming into Ames again."

"Things will get back to normal. Remember, there are still sane people here, it's just that the nutty ones are more visible right now."

Agnes held her nose and backed out the door. "Can't stand the smell anymore. And by the way, Summer, I had to take my dress down and have it let out." She pointed to her belly, which was significantly larger than I remembered it from the last time I'd seen her.

"Wow, Agnes. How many months are you?"

"Doctor says nearly five now. I guess I miscalculated at the beginning."

"Only four months until the baby comes? I can't believe it!"

"It kind of makes me wonder about the honeymoon."

"Why?"

"I don't know—it seems weird to be fooling around now, even though Sam seems to think I'm way sexier than I've ever been."

I laughed. "You're definitely more voluptuous, a word I never thought I'd use to describe you. Enjoy the attention—soon you'll have a screaming hungry baby with diapers to change."

"Thanks a lot for the support. I have no idea what to expect or how I'll deal with it."

"You have Sam to help and a good doctor, not to mention me, a designated auntie. You'll do just fine."

The wedding was the following weekend and I hoped we would have the case wrapped by then, but so far even with the database at his fingertips, Jerry had not discovered anything about Harry Dreiser. It was like the guy didn't exist. Sarah and I had both spent time with the sketch artist, the drawings of the man she dated and my vision of the shooter remarkably similar. Sarah had been shocked into silence when I told her about her father's double life.

"Are you absolutely certain?" she finally asked. "All I remember of him was a gentle and kind man who loved my mother."

"I'm sure he was that way, Sarah, it's just that he was also kind and gentle with another woman as well. I bet if we looked into it we'd find there are more stories like this than we realize. A lot of men just don't have it in them to spend their entire lives with one woman."

"What about my case? I just got a visit from another lawyer who promised to do well by me. He seemed competent and at least believed what I told him."

"I'm hoping you won't have to go to trial. Jerry is hard at work trying to find that man who called himself John Smith. He's your half-brother, Sarah."

Sarah made a face, the pale skin around her lips pinching in distaste. "Ugh. Thank the lord I didn't sleep with him."

"Did you almost—?"

Sarah nodded, her skin flushing. "He came onto me but I just didn't feel that way about him. But aside from that he didn't seem angry or even weird. Why would he shoot up the school?"

"That's what we're trying to find out, but first we have to locate him."

"I'm so sick of being in here," she said, looking around at the gray cement walls.

I patted her arm. "You'll be out soon, I promise. Just give us a few more days. Jerry is about to get in touch with the FBI since none of his other searches have revealed anything."

"And what about Lucille, my aunt? Maybe you should talk with her again—perhaps her nephew has been to see her."

"That's a good idea. I can call and ask the woman at the desk. She would know. And by the way, his real name is Harry Dreiser. Does that mean anything to you?"

"Harry Dreiser." Sarah stared into the distance. "No. I don't think I've heard that name before."

On my way out I saw the chief eyeing me with a nasty expression on her face. I tried not to let it bother me and turned away from her hostile stare. When I reached my car I was shaking.

I was fixing a spicy one-pot meal with chicken, sweet potatoes and spinach when I heard the door open. "Hey," I called, turning back to the mole` spices I was adding to the pan. "Were you able to find out anything?"

Jerry came into the kitchen, his lips brushing the back of my neck. "It's certainly weird being back at the police station. The chief is hostile as hell and quite a few of the force are on her side. It isn't what I'd call a serene environment." Jerry pulled open the refrigerator and grabbed a beer.

"But what about Harry Dreiser?"

"I've got an FBI agent looking into it—thank goodness I have a connection with Myra Proctor."

"She's helping?"

"She gave me the name of an agent, if that's what you mean. She's on our side."

I put the lid on the pan and turned from the stove. "That's good. Did you see her again?"

Jerry smirked. "Jealous?" He tipped his beer up and took a long pull.

"No, I'm not jealous—should I be?" I stared at him.

He laughed and grabbed me by the arm, pulling me to him. "You have to ask?"

When his cell phone rang he let me go to pull it out of his pocket. "Yeah," he said into the phone before he glanced at me and left the kitchen, taking his beer with him. He opened the front door and headed outside. I watched him through the window over the sink, wondering who he was talking to. His brows were furrowed in concentration and then his lips were moving, but since I couldn't read lips I had no idea what he was saying.

While I waited for him to come back inside I fed Cutty and the two cats who seemed to be fast friends now. Even Cutty seemed to have settled down about the new arrangement, allowing the cats to go about their business. I was still waiting for Jerry when I heard his motorcycle start up and then the sound of the engine as he roared away. What the hell? My cell phone rang a moment later and I went to grab it out of my purse.

"Did Jerry tell you?" Agnes asked.

"Tell me what?"

"Sam had a tip that Harry Dreiser might still be out in the woods."

"Who said that?"

"Anonymous. In any case Jerry and Sam are headed out there right now."

"He just took off on his bike and didn't say a word."

"Maybe he didn't want you to come along. According to Sam this could be dangerous, especially if the guy who called it in is setting a trap."

"Agnes, I don't like this."

"Neither do I. Should I come over?"

"Please do."

Fifteen minutes later Agnes arrived looking flustered and upset. I opened the door to let her in and then picked up Jerry's beer bottle off the stoop. "Why didn't he just tell me what was going on? I hate it when he does stuff like this."

Agnes went into the kitchen and lifted the lid on my stew. "This smells good."

"Want some? It's ready." I dished out two bowls and gave her one before collecting silverware from the drawer. "Who do you think called?" I asked, sitting next to her.

"Sam thinks it might have been Harry Dreiser himself. Maybe he feels guilty and wants to be caught."

"You could be right. If he's the author of those journals the guy is seriously disturbed. I just hope he isn't planning to kill them too."

Agnes blanched. "Don't say that! My wedding is in four days and I need a groom."

"Sorry, Agnes." I looked at her closely, noticing the bloom of color in her normally pale cheeks, the general look of health. "You look good."

Agnes finished chewing and put her spoon down. "I feel fantastic. I guess it's the hormones."

"Pregnancy agrees with you."

Agnes laughed. "Sam is so cute about it. He does

everything for me now, even cooking. He can't wait for the baby to be born, although he did mention—umm—"

"Sex?"

"He's nervous about the last few months and how we'll manage it. He has come up with some rather unique techniques lately, though—since his arm was injured. "

I had an image of myself naked wearing a cowboy hat. "Really? Like what?"

Agnes actually blushed. "Me on top, you know?"

"Yes, I do know," I answered, trying to keep the color from rising into my own cheeks.

"So you and Jerry—?"

I breathed a sigh of relief that Sam had not shared what he'd seen. "We do it like that sometimes."

"I like it because I'm more in control. And Sam likes it because he says he can look at me." She giggled.

I nodded and picked up our empty dishes and deposited them in the dishwasher. "I hope they call soon. I'm getting nervous."

Agnes jumped up, her face crumpling. "And here I am talking about our sex life. You've been out there, right? Maybe we should go. If Sam gets hurt I'll never forgive myself."

"What do you have to do with it? He's a cop, Agnes. But I'll drive us out if you really want to go."

Agnes nodded. "I really do."

I had a feeling this was a bad idea as I drove my car up the familiar gravel road. Agnes was pregnant and I had no business taking her with me, but when I asked her to wait in the car she gave me a look that would stop a fire in its tracks.

I parked down the hill from where Jerry and I had first gone into the woods. The moon was coming up over the dark forest, four days away from full. The wedding would be on full moon night, something Agnes had planned. I slipped the small pistol from the glove compartment and dropped it into my bag, glad that Jerry had insisted I have one, and then grabbed my flashlight. "Follow me and don't make any noise," I whispered.

"Where's Sam's car?"

I shrugged. "Maybe they went to a different area." The pale dogwood blossoms loomed out of the darkness as we approached the trees. I worked my way by them, trying to find the trail we'd followed before. I didn't want to use the flashlight unless I had to, afraid that if someone were lurking around they'd see the light.

"Why don't you turn on the flashlight?" Agnes hissed behind me.

I shook my head and kept going, wondering why in hell I'd agreed to this. I stopped and turned. "This is a bad idea," I whispered.

Her face looked very white in the darkness. "Did you have a premonition?"

"No. I just think—" When I heard a noise I grabbed Agnes and pulled her to a crouch next to me. "That's why," I whispered in her ear. We waited there listening for several very long moments before I stood and pulled her up. "Stay or go?" I asked, staring into the pools of her dark eyes.

"Stay."

I let out a long sigh and headed away again, following the narrow trail we'd been on before. When we reached the hill I'd climbed earlier I looked around, checking for my ghost, but he wasn't there. The detritus was deep around our feet and rustled loudly as we worked our way up the hill. At the top I stopped to listen again. When the ghost appeared out of the darkness I heard Agnes suck in her breath. I grabbed her arm.

"Quiet," I hissed. The ghost watched us and then moved away. "He wants us to follow," I whispered. "Are you up for this?"

Agnes nodded, her eyes wide.

The ghost led us up one hill and down the other, checking over his shoulder every so often to see if we were still there. We finally arrived at a rocky outcropping with a cave-like crevasse that led into darkness. When I turned to find him he had disappeared.

"I'm not going in there," Agnes hissed.

I turned on my flashlight and crawled through the narrow opening, shining it ahead as I pulled myself through. A second later I heard Agnes behind me. "What are you doing?" I whispered.

"I'm not staying out there alone."

I continued on, shining my light from side to side and noticing what looked like petroglyphs on the damp rock walls. I scraped my knee on some sharp stones and shone the light down to see what it was. "Someone's been living in here," I whispered, pointing to the remnants of a fire. I crawled deeper into the cave, glad when it opened out. But then my flashlight sputtered and went out. Agnes grabbed my shirt, her frightened whisper reverberating off the stone.

"Let's go back!"

"Just a second," I said, feeling in front of me. My fingers came into contact with something smooth and cold. I held it close to my face and dropped it, adrenaline coursing through my body.

"What is it?"

"I think it's a human femur."

Agnes moaned. "Please, Summer. Let's go."

I fiddled with my flashlight, shaking it and trying it again. When it came on it blinded me for a second. Agnes screamed.

In front of us was a human skeleton wearing a tattered uniform straight out of WW2, a sheet of weathered paper held between skeletal fingers. I pulled at it until it came loose and held it up to the light.

God forgive me for what I've done.

Signed, Harry Dreiser

"Agnes, this is the shooter. This is Harry Dreiser."

"Whoever it is, he's long dead. Please get me out of here."

Agnes and I made our way out of the woods and back to the car without saying one word. Once we were inside my Honda and rolling down the hill toward home, Agnes turned her tear-streaked face my way. "That was the creepiest thing I've ever seen in my life. How long do you think he's been there?"

"I don't know. If he's really the shooter I thought it took longer to end up without any meat on your bones."

Agnes shuddered. "Don't talk about it."

When we got back to the house Jerry's motorcycle was parked in the alley, Sam's police car next to it. I pulled up in back of Agnes's Fiat and cut the engine. A second later the door flew open and Sam rushed out, Jerry on his heels.

"Where in hell have you two been?" Jerry shouted.

I looked at Sam who was embracing Agnes, a look of relief on his face. "That's a better way to greet the woman you love," I said, pointing.

Jerry grabbed me roughly and pulled me into his arms. "Jesus Christ, woman. Where did you go? We were worried sick."

I pulled back. "I found him, Jerry. I found Harry Dreiser."

"What? I thought Sam and I found him."

I stared at him and then noticed my neighbor watching us. "Let's go inside."

The four of us settled around the table in the kitchen.

"Okay, let's start at the beginning," Jerry said, his brown eyes focused on mine. "Tell us what happened."

After I finished with my gruesome depiction of events Jerry glanced at Sam. "What the hell is going on?"

Sam raised his eyebrows and held his hands out palms up. "Don't know, man."

"What did you two find?"

"We found a dead body in a hollow next to where we found those newspaper clippings and the journal. We called it in and the ME met us out there."

"I guess the ME should get the skeleton too, don't you think?"

Jerry glanced quickly toward Sam and turned back to me. "Yeah, unless you were hallucinating."

"Jerry! That's uncalled for," I said, frowning. "Agnes saw him too."

"I didn't mean hallucinating exactly—I just thought he might be a ghost."

"It wasn't a ghost," Agnes whispered, leaning into Sam next to her. "We saw one of those earlier."

"A ghost led us to the body, Jerry. And look at this." I pulled the brittle piece of paper out of my jacket pocket and handed it to him.

Jerry read it and handed it to Sam who rose and pulled out his cell phone. "Can you describe where he is?" Sam asked me. "I'm hoping I can catch the ME before he leaves the woods. No point in him making two trips."

I did the best I could, hoping they would discover the cave. "It's down from that hill, you know, where all the rocks are?"

Sam seemed to understand where I meant. He punched in the numbers and headed into the living room to give directions.

"What was your body like?" I asked Jerry.

"Very dead and very pungent. But he isn't skeletal like yours apparently is."

"Ours was wearing an old WW2 uniform," Agnes added.

"Maybe he was the father or the grandfather." Jerry gazed at me.

I shook my head. "They both died overseas. I think Harry Dreiser found an old uniform that belonged to his father or grandfather and put it on before he shot up the school."

Jerry frowned. "I'm not sure I buy that."

"He was in Sarah's house, Jerry. I bet some uniforms and other war stuff are stored there. He had plenty of opportunity. Have a cop check on her house. Why do you think your body is the right body?"

Jerry scoffed. "I didn't think it was a contest. Sam and I found a dead guy who we assumed was Dreiser. We can match Sarah's DNA with the two stiffs and see which one is a match."

"Ugh," Agnes muttered. "You guys are so gross."

Sam walked into the kitchen and sat next to Agnes. "The ME hopes to find dead guy number two, but he isn't promising anything. I don't think the ghost is going to help him."

"Should we go back and lead them there?" I asked.

Jerry gazed at me and then looked at his partner. "Why don't you take Agnes home and Summer and I will finish up. Just give them a call and tell them we're coming."

We all shuffled out the front door, Agnes and Sam heading to the cruiser. Jerry followed me to my car and climbed into the passenger seat. "What a night," he muttered, staring at the moon.

I started my car, put it in first and eased out the clutch. "I can't believe we both found bodies. I wonder who yours is?"

Jerry laughed. "I was wondering who yours is."

"Jerry, I'm sure he's Harry. The ghost showed us where to look."

"The ghost could have his own motivations."

"Oh please."

By the time we got home it was close to midnight. I felt a sense of relief now that I knew my skeleton would soon be on his way to the morgue. We would have answers very soon.

24

I was lying awake next to Jerry when my dog sat up and pricked his ears toward the open bedroom door. "What is it?" I whispered, trying not to wake Jerry. But my cop boyfriend slept like a dead man, only waking to an alarm or an extremely loud noise. I left the warm bed and crept into the living room, not surprised to see Sadie Cumberland standing there. "You found the secret," she said softly. "The circle is complete."

"Harry Dreiser—is he the secret?"

Sadie nodded and tried to touch me, but her hand went right through my arm. "Grant tried to stop him but he wasn't strong enough." She slowly faded away until all I could see was her shining hair—and then even that was gone. I thought I heard her whisper, *I'm so sorry,* and then I was alone in a cold living room. I shivered and hurried back to bed.

In the morning over coffee I told Jerry about Sadie. "She said 'the circle is complete'. I wonder what she meant."

Jerry grinned. "Maybe it's a ghost thing."

"She also said that Grant tried to stop him—how can a ghost stop a man from shooting up a school?"

"Obviously he can't." Jerry rose and put two pieces of whole grain bread into the toaster.

"When will they have the DNA results?"

"Maybe today."

"We still don't know why he did it, Jerry. I wish we had the whole story."

"Unless he comes to you and explains, I guess we never will."

"Do you think Harry Dreiser is my guy or yours?"

"I don't know, Summer, and I really don't care as long as one of them is."

"I really hope we get closure on this. It's frustrating not to be able to talk to the shooter."

Jerry headed toward the front door. "Don't think too hard about it. I'll call as soon as I find something out."

I stood. "Aren't you going to kiss me goodbye?"

"What are you, the little wifey?" Jerry smirked and opened the door. "See you later, Mrs. Cleaver."

"Very funny!" I yelled.

I was talking with a contractor at Tarot and Tea when my cell phone rang. "Can you excuse me for a moment?" I asked, grabbing my purse. I pulled out my phone and slid my finger across the screen. "What did you find out?"

"It's your guy, Summer. He's related to Sarah. And there's more. They found other stuff in the cave."

"What other stuff?"

"I'll tell you later. I've got to go."

I was finishing up with Dale when Douglas wandered in.

"Have you solved the case?"

I looked around to see if Dale or his assistant were within earshot. "I found a body and Jerry says it's him."

"Who exactly?"

"Harry Dreiser. He's Sarah's half-brother who she

216

never knew about."

"And you think he's the shooter?"

"Isn't he?"

Douglas smiled. "How would I know?"

I watched him leave the store, this time seeing him open the door and move through it. But when I looked out the glass at the top, checking for his figure on the street, there was no one there.

"What did you have in mind for the bookshelves, Ms McCloud?" Dale asked, pulling my thoughts back to the problem at hand.

After Dale and his men left I called Jerry. "Tell me what you have," I asked.

"I have a splitting headache and an uncommon hatred for the chief who seems to think if she outstares me she'll win some contest."

"Ha ha—very funny. Can you please tell me what they found in the cave?"

"Letters, Summer. Lots and lots of letters."

"Between?"

"Between Harry Dreiser and Lucille, between Timothy and Grant and between Sadie and Grant and between Carol and Lucille. It's a slam dunk now."

"A slam dunk? You mean that Harry did this terrible thing?"

"I'd say an emphatic yes."

"So who is the guy you and Sam found?"

"Apparently he's a homeless dude who got killed by one of those vigilantes. He was shot in the head at close range. We're checking ballistics and we hope to find whoever did it. To tell you the truth I'd like to round all of them up and throw them behind bars."

"But who called you to send you out there?"

There was a long silence. "You tell me."

"A ghost? You think a ghost called you?"

"I don't know, but I'd believe just about anything after what we've been through."

That night after dinner Jerry handed over a folder of evidence. "I shouldn't do this now that I'm on the payroll again, but since you've been so involved I thought I should share these with you."

I took it with me to the couch and pulled out a stack of letters secured with a rubber band. I removed one and reached into the envelope, settling back to read.

Dear Aunt Lucille,

I can't stand it anymore. I feel like if I don't do something soon I'll lose my mind. You know what I've been through, you know how my mother died. How would you feel? I know you won't approve of what I have planned but I can't turn back now. My life is over and this will cinch it. Please forgive me.

Your loving nephew,

Harry

I pulled put another one, opening the brittle paper carefully. It was several newspaper articles paper-clipped together. The headline of one read:

Carol Dreiser commits suicide in front of her son. Carol Dreiser, a woman well known in Providence for her singing voice, has died. According to her twelve-year-old son, Harry Dreiser, she put a rope around her neck and jokingly told him to pull the chair out from under her. Thinking it was a prank he did as she asked. The boy has been taken to the hospital and will be in the psych ward for at least a week until a foster family can be provided.

Some notes had been written in the margins: *She*

died because of the war. She died because of me. Why did she have to die? I hate them all.

"Did you read any of these?" I asked Jerry, feeling sick at heart.

Jerry nodded, coming over to sit next to me. "Hard stuff. The kid was broken early in life and never recovered."

"Do you think he confused the school with the recruitment office?"

Jerry reached over and riffled through the letters and pulled one out. "Read this one."

I opened the paper.

Dear Aunt Lucille,

I continue to watch the recruitment center, wondering why so many kids are going in and out. I'd rather not kill them along with the bastards who ruined my life, but if I have to I will. My plan is to make a statement about the war and how it has ruined so many lives. So much death and destruction—so much pain, my mother's included. She was never the same after my father was killed in the war. And now she's dead too.

"He thought the school was still a recruitment center?"

Jerry nodded. "Apparently he wasn't all there. We've spoken with the hospital that kept him when he was young and their records indicate he was severely damaged by what happened to his mother and his part in it. His hallucinations must have begun recently because before that he visited Lucille, and according to her and the manager, seemed like a normal human being."

"What was the trigger?"

"That Thompson machine gun."

I stared at Jerry. "How do you know?"

"I just do."

Jerry wouldn't say something like this lightly. He'd gone through enough therapy himself to understand the psychological ins and outs of mental problems. I figured he was right. "Has Sarah been released?"

"She will be as soon as the paperwork gets sorted. Myra has taken over until we can find a new chief."

"Will you be the new chief?"

Jerry shook his head. "I have no desire to be chief—I never did. I like being a homicide detective and having you as my sidekick."

"Batman and Robin?"

"I think we need to come up with our very own definition—maybe ghost buster and idiot, or something along those lines."

"How about Smartman and woman who talks to ghosts?"

Jerry laughed.

"Speaking of—where are Mischief and Tabby?" I put the folder down on the coffee table and called for my kitties in my sweet kitty-calling voice. I heard a sound and then a large basket on the shelf above my stove moved. A second later it tumbled down and Mischief and Tabby both fell out. "What? You guys are fast friends now?" Mischief marched to his food dish with his tail in the air. "Ok, Ok, I'll feed you," I laughed. I scooped the nasty smelling fishy pate out of the can on the counter and plopped it into his dish, adding some to Tabby's dish as well.

When I came back to the couch Jerry was reading another letter. "Do you think Harry knew that Sarah was his half-sister?" I asked.

He put the letter down. "I don't know. Didn't you say he wanted to have sex with Sarah? That makes me think he didn't."

"So he just happens to run into this woman who just happens to be his half-sister? And then he sees this machine gun that belonged to his grandfather that he ends up stealing?"

"I don't know. We may never know unless he wrote something down about it—but so far I haven't seen anything."

"Do you know how he died?"

"Bullet to the back of the brain with that Colt you and I found."

"He shot himself in the back of the head? How is that possible?"

Jerry stared into the distance, his gaze clouding. "Odd thing that. And the only fingerprints we found on the revolver belonged to Timothy Cumberland."

25

It was two days later that Sarah was released. Unfortunately on her way out of the police station she was attacked by an angry mob and had to be taken to the hospital in an ambulance. The good news was that all of the attackers were summarily rounded up and placed in jail cells. Jerry had his wish, at least for the moment.

I drove to the hospital early the next morning hoping she would be released in time for Agnes's wedding the next afternoon. When I came into her room my heart sank. She was pale as paper, her eyes sunken and dull.

"How are you feeling?" I asked, sitting in the chair next to the bed.

"I've been better. The good news is I only have a slight concussion. I should get out today."

I picked up her limp hand. "I'm so sorry you've had to go through all this. It all should have been cleared up weeks ago."

Sarah tried to smile. "At least they didn't kill me."

I shook my head, feeling the weight of her pain and distress come down on my shoulders. "They're all in jail."

Sarah raised herself up for a second and then fell back. "For how long? Will I ever get my life back?"

"As soon as the local newspaper prints the truth things should begin to calm down. And according to Jerry there will be a trial. They killed a homeless man out in the woods."

"See? They are crazy. I don't trust these people any more. They want vengeance and it doesn't matter whether they hurt innocent people in the process. I've decided to move away from here. I don't want to live in that house with all the memories and the crap my parents left behind. And I have no living relatives to keep me around."

"You have Lucille, your aunt. She's all alone now that Harry's gone."

Sarah gazed at me. "I do have to go and talk with her about all this. But after that I—"

"Try not to make any hasty decisions. A lot has happened and you need time to process it all."

"I guess you're right about that." Sarah turned away, her eyes filling with tears.

"I want you to come to the wedding. Agnes is expecting you."

Sarah shook her head. "I can't, Summer. I'd just bring everybody down."

"I insist and I won't take no for an answer. I'll come over and pick you up and bring you home afterwards."

I left a few minutes later with the promise to meet her at her house on Sunday afternoon at three. The wedding would take place at four-thirty, the reception from six on, but I was the maid of honor and had to be there to help with any last minute details. On the way out of the hospital a man hurried by me heading inside. When I glanced at him I was sure he had the same jawline as the Cumberland men, but when I turned to see where he'd gone there was no one in the hallway.

I was dressed in my new black dress, my hair arranged by a hairdresser and piled on top of my head. My black heels hurt my feet but I decided to ignore it. The night before I'd had the rehearsal dinner at my house and met Sam's brother, David, for the first time, a Universal Life minister who would be officiating. I also met Sam's parents, a waspish couple who seemed annoyed by my house and me. Douglas had engaged them in conversation as only Douglas could. But when their attitude about the pregnancy came clear, Agnes's father became incensed. They had embarrassed Agnes by their disapproving glances and the whispering they did between themselves before we sat down to dinner. At one point Agnes had been in the bathroom in tears, me trying to calm her down.

When she got back to the table, her face red from crying, Sam had stood up and raised his glass. "To our marriage and to our baby," he said strongly, staring down his parents. "Anyone who doesn't feel excited and pleased by our news can go away now, because we want only joy and happiness on our special day."

Right after that Douglas stood up and raised his glass. "To my daughter and her soon-to-be husband, Sam, as well as my upcoming grandchild. I couldn't be happier."

The rest of the group joined him in his toast, even Sam's parents who looked abashed. The rest of the evening went smoothly but I was happy when it was over. Jerry helped me clean up and then the two of us fell into bed exhausted.

When I picked up Sarah, she looked a lot better than I expected her to. Somehow she'd found time to dye her roots, her hair a color between old oak leaves and mahogany. She was dressed in pale green linen, a color that suited her and she'd applied make-up. Her cheeks were rosy, her lips painted a tasteful color of pale pink. There was an excited expression in her eyes that I'd never seen.

"I shouldn't have let you talk me into this," she said, following me to the car. "I'm not sure I can remember how to have a civil conversation with regular people."

I smiled. "It's like riding a bicycle. It will be good for you to be around people, especially the ones who are coming together to celebrate Agnes and Sam. Jerry's the best man and you'll recognize customers from Tarot and Tea."

"I was sorry to hear what happened to your store, Summer. What has this town come to?"

I shrugged. "It's being fixed up and I should be able to open up in a few weeks. I'm putting it all behind me just as you need to put your jail time behind you."

We pulled up in front of the beautifully refurbished Victorian, got out of the car and headed inside.

26

David stood at the front of what had originally been a dining room under a set of enormous gilt-framed mirrors, his hands folded sedately in front of him. He looked a lot like Sam with his blonde hair and blue eyes, but being the eldest he had a more serious edge to him, frown lines marring his forehead. I stood on one side with Jerry across from me, Sam in the middle facing out and waiting for his bride. When Jerry's and my eyes met for an instant I saw something in his glance that gave me a fluttery feeling. He looked very handsome in his tux.

I took one last look around the room, admiring the bouquets of flowers at the end of each row of chairs, the tables in the back with vases full of birds of paradise, tall purple lupine and lacy greenery. All my doing. Light streamed in through the clearstory windows, the coved twelve-foot high ceiling alive with flickering shadows cast by maple, oak and birch leaves moving in the light breeze. The room was filled to capacity with standing room only, the soft murmur of voices quickly coming to an end when the piano began. Agnes's friend Frankie was the pianist, a slight girl whose nimble fingers picked out the wedding march with enthusiasm.

I heard Sam gasp when Agnes appeared at the back of the room on Douglas's arm. She did look amazing in her gray dress, the sparkling band that came across her forehead and bangs. I'd lent her the borrowed and blue part of her outfit, a tiny bracelet of turquoise beads my mother had given me years before. The old was the dress, the new was her headband—all was as it should be, I assured the superstitious part of myself.

Everyone rose as they walked toward us along the aisle between the chairs. When they reached us Douglas kissed her cheek and left her next to Sam who couldn't seem to take his eyes off her. I understood why. She glanced at me and handed me her bouquet.

The hand written vows had been solemnly spoken, the beautifully designed rings produced by Jerry and given, before I noticed that Douglas was sitting next to a familiar woman. Serena was wearing a sparkling silvery twenties style dress that went well with the dress Agnes wore, a band in her dark hair as well. I'd never noticed how much they looked alike until that moment. Of course it had been a couple of years since I'd seen Serena, and with her theatrical background she was a master of disguise. All I knew was that she looked remarkably well for being a ghost, and I could see the expression of love with which Douglas regarded her, his eyes bright.

I was in the ballroom drinking a glass of champagne waiting for the bride and groom to appear when Jerry came close, his hand moving to my waist. "That was a seriously fine wedding. When we decide—" But he stopped in mid-sentence when Sam and Agnes entered the room, their mutual happiness shining on their faces.

"May I present Mr. and Mrs. Anderson," Douglas announced, standing aside. The room erupted in cheers, catcalls and hoots and then everyone surged forward to congratulate them, Jerry and me included.

Agnes and Sam were milling through the guests receiving their blessings when I saw Serena head toward her daughter. Agnes looked shocked when she saw her, the two women facing each other for several long moments before Serena pulled her daughter into her arms. When I looked again Agnes was crying, streaks of mascara on her face. By the time I hurried over Serena was talking with Douglas and drinking a glass of champagne.

"You need to freshen up," I said in my maid of honor voice. I grabbed her by the arm and dragged her to the bathroom. By the time we got there Agnes had stopped crying but I could feel the tremble in her as she stared into the mirror.

"That was my mother," she said shakily. "My mother is a ghost and she came to my wedding. She hugged me, Summer. She felt as solid as you do."

I nodded, helping her wash off the mascara. "You two look so much alike. Did you notice her dress?"

Agnes turned to stare at me. "How does a ghost come up with that outfit?"

"She probably owned it in the twenties. And did you forget that Douglas is also a ghost?"

Agnes let out a sigh and dabbed some powder she took from my make-up bag on her nose. "I'm used to him—I don't think of him like that."

"This is the first time Serena's appeared since her death. She came for you."

Agnes's eyes widened. "Don't say that—it gives me a creepy feeling."

"Why?"

"Because she's dead, Summer!" she shouted just as another woman entered the bathroom.

She stared at the two of us and hurried into a stall.

"Do you know her?" I mouthed.

Agnes shook her head. "Sam's crew. Let's get out of here."

I was dancing with Jerry to the sound of the quartet that had set up on the patio when I saw Serena and Douglas head outside together. "I wonder where they're going," I whispered, pointing.

"Maybe to rekindle their love affair," Jerry whispered, his breath warm on my neck.

"I think it's more likely that Douglas wants to talk to her about Agnes. My friend doesn't seem that happy to have her dead mother show up at her wedding."

Jerry chuckled. "I hope to hell my father never comes back. I think I'd have to kill him if he did."

I laughed but I wondered why some people came back and others didn't. It seemed so random and strange.

As Jerry swung me around I noticed Sarah dancing with a handsome older man. "Who's that?" I asked.

"Never seen him before but I noticed Douglas introducing them earlier."

"Oh god. I hope he isn't a ghost. By the way, what ever happened with Harry Dreiser's letters? Did you find out anything else?"

Jerry pulled back to look at me. "Didn't I tell you? The ME said there was no way his body could have deteriorated that quickly. According to him Harry would have had to be out there for years to end up in that condition. He figured the guy had been there for ten years or more—he estimated his age was between forty and sixty. "

"What are you saying?"

Jerry cast a glance toward Sarah and her brown-haired partner. "The guy in the cave wasn't Harry."

"But if that wasn't Harry where is he? And what about the fingerprints on the gun?"

"I can't explain it and neither can anyone else. But we have the confession in the form of letters as well as that note. At least we got Sarah off the hook." Jerry shrugged, looking over again at Sarah and her partner who were now walking out of the room. They looked pretty friendly to have just met. Sarah turned as they were going out the door, her gaze meeting mine. She waved and smiled.

I couldn't believe Jerry would let this go and not even question whether we had the right guy. Something seemed off to me. "Who is that man?" I muttered, straining to see where they were going.

"Can't you relax and enjoy the reception? Did you see the layout of food over there?" He pointed to a long table covered in dishes of salmon, several salads and asparagus, people moving along it with plates in their hands.

"I'm the person who organized the caterers—Saffron and Seaweed. It should be good for how much it cost." I wriggled away from him. "I need to ask Douglas about that man Sarah is with. Can you excuse me for a second?" I hurried into the garden. When I found Douglas he was alone, walking along one of the pebbled paths with his hands behind his back, a look of sadness on his features.

I fell into step beside him. "Where's Serena?"

He turned his dark eyes to mine. "She only came for the wedding."

"I'm sorry to hear that, Douglas."

He nodded, looking down. "I was surprised and pleased to see her but I have no idea if or when it will happen again."

I put my hand on his arm. "Who was the man Sarah was dancing with? Jerry said you introduced them?"

Douglas looked surprised. "I didn't introduce them. I assumed he was an old friend of Sarah's."

I stared at him. He must know more than that, but the look on his face said something else. "You don't have any idea who he is?"

Douglas shook his head. "My thoughts have been with Serena and Agnes and Sam and this celebration. If Sarah has a new beau I say good for her. It isn't any of my concern."

I looked around for Sarah, spotting her on the far side of the garden under a tree. She and the brown-haired man were kissing and it lasted a lot longer than any friendly kiss should last. I was about to head toward them when Jerry came up behind me.

"Summer? What are you doing? I went to get you a glass of champagne and you disappeared." He handed me a crystal flute filled to the brim with golden bubbly liquid.

"Douglas says he didn't introduce that guy to Sarah and I just saw them kissing."

"So? Isn't Sarah allowed to have fun for a change?"

"It's not that—it's just that he reminds me of the pictures I've seen of the Cumberland family. If that guy in the woods wasn't Harry then maybe this guy—" I thought of the man who had gone by me on my way out of the hospital, turning to where they'd been a moment before, but Sarah and her guy were no longer there.

Jerry grabbed my arm. "Come and mingle, Summer. It's time to let this case go. Sarah's free now and we have a body and a confession—isn't that enough?"

I let him lead me toward a crowd of people chatting and laughing, the spicy aroma of roses filling my nostrils.

The sun was warm on my head and arms and I had a pleasant buzz from the champagne. Ahead of me I could see Agnes, her head thrown back in a laugh, Sam looking down on her adoringly. I turned again to see where Sarah had gone, my attention taken by a couple getting into a black sedan at the front of the building.

"She's leaving," I said, grabbing Jerry's sleeve, "and that guy's with her."

Jerry followed my gaze. "What is with you? Maybe they're planning to go have sex or something. Just because she's in her sixties doesn't mean she…"

"I know that," I snapped. "It's just that he could be Harry."

Jerry stared at me, his eyes wide. "You've been convinced all this time that Sarah didn't do this and now you think she and Harry plotted the entire thing?"

I shook the wayward thoughts out of my mind and tried to laugh. "You're right, it's ridiculous." I followed him over to where my best friend and Sam were about to cut the four-tiered cake. The tiny bride and groom perched on the top were replicas of Sam and Agnes, the groom blonde-haired, the bride with black. I wasn't sure who was responsible for this, but I thought it a sweet detail. Sam and Agnes held the knife and cut it together and then fed each other the first pieces before opening it up to the rest of the crowd, half of whom were still stuffing themselves with the delectable buffet.

"Want some food?" Jerry asked.

I followed him to the table and picked up a plate.

27

It was two days later that I thought I'd check on Sarah. I hadn't seen or heard from her since the wedding. Agnes and Sam were off on their honeymoon and Jerry was working. I had little to occupy myself other than overseeing the construction at Tarot and Tea.

I pulled up in front of Sarah's house and parked the car, my mind on my store and the need to make sure that what was happening was exactly what I wanted. When I knocked on Sarah's door I was miles away. It was several minutes before I knocked again and when no one answered I turned the knob, surprised to find it unlocked. "Sarah!" I called out walking inside. The house was dark and smelled musty, the curtains pulled over all the windows. "Sarah!" I called again moving into the living room. In the middle of the room was a glass coffee table empty of anything except a heavy paperweight that held down a white sheet of paper. I moved the glass piece aside and picked up the paper, surprised to see it addressed to me.

Dear Summer,
I'm sorry I didn't get a chance to say goodbye. As you know I planned to leave Ames after everything that happened. But circumstances have sent me away even earlier than I'd planned. You see, I lied to you about the person I referred to as John Smith, afraid if I were honest

you would be horrified. His real name is Harry Dreiser, my half-brother, but despite the taboo we are in love and have been for a while. And since we are too old to have children we decided that to stay apart was folly. Harry has explained to me that he is not responsible for the shooting and I have to believe him. As far as the weapon and the fingerprints, I am mystified, but I know it was not Harry who did this awful deed. He is a kind and gentle soul who adores me. Please do not try and find us. Thank you for all the work you did on my behalf. I owe you everything for getting me out of that jail cell. I now have a life to live and a man I love to live it with.

I will never return to this house so as far as I'm concerned you are welcome to open it up to anyone who would care to use the furnishings. As far as my father and grandfather's uniforms and other wartime artifacts, please give them to charity or a museum.

Sarah Cumberland

I stared at the note in my hand, my thoughts whirling in every direction. I reached into my pocket for my cell phone and called Jerry.

"I'm in Sarah's house. She's gone and guess who's with her?"

"Is this a trick question?"

"Harry Dreiser is with her. That's the man she was with at the wedding."

There was a moment of silence as Jerry digested this. "I'll put a bolo out."

A second later he hung up without even saying goodbye. I wandered around the house looking in closets and finding uniforms and memorabilia from the Second World War, my thoughts cascading from one scenario to the next. The ME hadn't identified the skeleton other than saying it was an 85% DNA match to Sarah Cumberland. We still didn't know if it was Timothy or Grant. And how could it be either of them? Unless—unless the body had been brought back to the States and Harry had placed it in that cave and added the note to steer the police in the wrong direction. And if that were the case it was a set-up from the very beginning. We needed to have a long talk with the ME.

Two weeks later Jerry still had found no trace of Sarah Cumberland or Harry Dreiser. It was like they had vanished from the face of the earth. When Jerry went to the bank to check on Sarah's accounts the officer told him that Sarah had closed out her checking and her savings, telling him that she planned to move to Barbados. But when Jerry checked the flights in and out of Providence, Hartford, Boston, and New York, neither Sarah nor Harry came up on the rosters, nor anyone who fit their description. Jerry had the police searching up and down the Eastern seaboard trying to locate them and had spoken with his contact at the FBI.

"What about false identities?" I asked him.

"Pretty hard to do now with Homeland Security breathing down our necks," Jerry answered. "But Harry Dreiser may be a lot more clever than we first imagined."

"We assumed he was shell-shocked and imagined it was still a recruitment center. All the shootings I've heard about were done by crazies who got their hands on a gun and went nuts."

Jerry shook his head. "There's always some motive unless the person is mentally ill, and from what we've discovered, I don't think this guy is."

"What about Sarah? Do you think she was involved? I'm pretty sure I saw Harry at the hospital the day before the wedding."

"I don't know if she was involved, but I'd guess no."

Several days later I took matters into my own hands and drove up to Providence, hoping that Lucille might know something. She was quite lucid the day I visited, her eyes bright.

"That dear boy was here not long ago. He told me he'd fallen in love. I am so pleased for him after everything he's been through."

"What happened to Timothy, Harry's father? Did his body get shipped back after the war?"

Lucille looked down, a frown further wrinkling her spotted skin. "We had a funeral for Timothy. And as I recall there was a coffin." She looked up, her eyes bright. "Yes, there definitely was a coffin and he was buried in the Ames graveyard, next to the old stone church."

"Did Harry mention the woman he'd fallen in love with?"

"He didn't mention her name but he warned me that I might not see him for quite a while, that he and his ladylove were taking some time together. After all, they aren't spring chickens," Lucille added with a raspy chuckle. "He mentioned going to a secret place where they could be entirely alone."

"Did he say where?"

Lucille smiled. "If he'd told me it wouldn't be a secret, would it?"

On the way home I called Jerry. "We need to check out the graveyard, Jerry—the one on the east side of town. Timothy was supposedly buried there."

"We've already established that Timothy was more than likely the body in that cave."

"But we don't know do we? If we dig up the coffin and there's no body in it we'll know for sure."

"The way things are at the station right now I don't think I could get the authorization."

"You won't have to if we do it."

There was a lengthy silence before Jerry said, "You're serious, aren't you?"

"It will prove that Harry planned the entire thing."

When we entered the graveyard through a little wooden gate two nights later and searched for Timothy Cumberland's grave I saw several ghosts rise up to take a look at us, but when I pointed them out to Jerry he couldn't see them. The graveyard was old with many graves dating back a hundred years, the little stone church abandoned years before. The night was black as pitch, clouds covering up any moonlight there might have been, and that coupled with the late hour and the ghosts lent a special ghoulishness to what we were up to.

When we finally found the grave and began to dig Jerry turned to me.

"Did you notice that the sod is two by two foot squares?" Jerry whispered, placing them carefully a distance away. It was important for us to put it back the way it was in order not to be arrested for grave robbing.

"Does that mean the grave's been disturbed recently?"

"I would definitely say it's been disturbed in the past few months," Jerry said, turning back to his work. He was knee deep in mud, his boots caked with the slimy red clay.

When I put my shovel in I noticed a glow to my left and turned to see a ghost sitting on a grave watching us. His outfit of dark waistcoat and top hat indicated that he'd lived in the eighteen hundreds. When he noticed me looking at him he doffed his hat and bowed, a wide grin on his nearly translucent face. "Jerry, can you see the ghost?" I asked, pulling on his sleeve.

"What ghost?" Jerry turned to where I pointed but my guy was gone.

"He was sitting on that grave stone watching us. Once we're done here I want to see who it belongs to." I turned back to my work.

My arms ached from digging when my shovel hit wood, the sound unmistakable. I was working more carefully when Jerry gave me a little push. I lost my balance and fell face down in the mud we'd stacked along the edges of the hole. And when I pushed myself up to my knees I realized my entire front body was covered in the slimy goo, including my hands. "Why did you do that?" I hissed.

When I tried to stand my foot slipped and I caught hold of Jerry's arm, bringing him down in the mud beside me. I waited for him to yell but when our eyes met he began to laugh and then both of us were choking with laughter as we tried to keep our voices down. Jerry looked like some kind of mud monster, his body covered in goo, his eyes dark and full of mirth.

The coffin was a simple one and not locked shut like so many of them. Jerry took out a tool from his jacket and pressed it into the cracks along the side to pry it open. When it finally gave he fell, muddying the back of his jeans. The casket was empty, aside from several rocks. He ignored the muck as he pulled gloves from his pocket and put them on over his mud-caked fingers. He removed the rocks and placed them in an evidence bag and then pulled out a DNA kit and swabbed out the inside of the coffin from one end to the other.

"You think Ray can get DNA from the coffin?"

Jerry glanced at me. "If the body was in here there

has to be DNA. I doubt whoever removed the body had the forethought to clean out the inside of the coffin. Unfortunately I can't use it without revealing what we did, which is highly illegal."

Once we'd shoveled the mud back into the grave and placed the sod carefully back and pressed it in place I went to take a look at the grave where the ghost had been sitting. The very old moss-covered stone read:

FINLAY ROSS MCCLOUD
AUGUST 17, 1789-SEPTEMBER 29,1884
TRUE LOVE LIVES ON

"Jerry, this is my relative," I said, pointing.

Jerry came over and held the tiny flashlight out. "Finlay Ross McCloud. How do you know?"

"Because my mother spoke of him. He was one of the first of the family to come here from Scotland. How could I forget a name like that?"

"We'll have to name our first born after him," Jerry whispered, turning away.

I caught my breath and stood stock-still. Did Jerry really just say that? I sighed and followed him out the little gate and up the hill toward where we'd parked the car. I wanted to bring it up on the way home but I couldn't find the words. I couldn't just ask if he was thinking about marrying me, could I? We'd never talked about getting married. After a few minutes of mulling it over I just figured it was an offhand comment that meant nothing.

We were nearing home when Jerry turned to me. "Why did you think I pushed you?"

I stared at him, trying to detect his expression in the dark. But all I could see was the mud on his cheek and the caked mud that had dried on his jacket. "Are you saying you didn't?"

"That's what I'm saying."

I looked out at the deserted streets, the soft rain that had just begun. I had definitely felt hands on me, Jerry's hands I'd assumed. If he hadn't done it then who had? Was it Finlay, my relative, who thought it would be funny to see me covered in mud? I shivered and moved closer.

I was at Tarot and Tea three weeks later when Jerry drove up on his bike. I was in conference with the contractor and wondered why he hadn't thought to call first. It was a hot July day and I was wearing a sundress, my feet bare, but when I looked around for my sandals I couldn't find them.

I watched him pull off his helmet and run his fingers through his hair, a frown on his face. He came up the steps two at a time to the open front door. It was repaired now, the splintered wood replaced with newly stained boards and varnished to a high gleam, my repainted *Tarot and Tea* sign above it. Before I could point out the repairs he grabbed my hand and dragged me away from the contractor and the other two men working inside. The grass was cool on my feet, my attention going to the feel of it tickling my toes as I followed him toward the sidewalk.

"The ME says the DNA on those rocks is an 85% match to the skeleton and to Sarah and to what he found on the jacket."

"In other words they're all related."

Jerry nodded. "And there's more. The swab from inside the coffin was a 100% match to the skeleton. It was definitely Timothy Cumberland in the cave. As you know, Ray had to send this off to a friend of his at a private lab and we can't use it—I swore him to secrecy about our grave robbing. I've thought long and hard about what to do about Harry and Sarah and I've spoken to Sam. We've alerted every police station from here to Canada and down as far as Mexico. The FBI has their pictures at every border of every state and every airport. If they show up with fake passports they will be caught."

"I wonder about the ghost who tried to stop Harry. Do you think he was involved with steering us in the wrong direction? Sadie said the circle is complete. What did she mean by that?"

Jerry stared at me. "Do we think it was Grant or Timothy who tried to stop Harry?"

I shrugged. "The guy who pointed me to the cave was too old to be Timothy, so I'm assuming Grant." I let out a little laugh. "It's like a ghost conspiracy has been trying to keep Harry from getting caught. Maybe they felt sorry for him after everything he went through."

Jerry stared into the distance. "The town went crazy before we arrested Sarah, and since we supposedly found the shooter dead in that cave with basically a signed confession in his bony fingers, everything has returned to normal. I am inclined to leave things as they are, especially since there is no trace of Harry and Sarah, and believe me I've tried every trick I know to find them, even to the point of pissing off several fellow officers. What do you think we should do?"

I gazed at him, surprised by the question. Jerry had never been one to stop short before—'no stone unturned' was his motto. I thought about it, not wanting to revisit the disturbing weeks before the wedding. From what I'd read in those letters and journal entries Harry Dreiser had experienced a lot of dark days. "After the torching of my shop, the vigilantes with guns combing through the forest, and the mob that attacked Sarah, I have to agree with you. If the media discovered the police had re-opened the case I hate to think what might happen."

Jerry nodded. "I'm glad you feel that way. See you at home?"

I stared down the street toward the bakery. I hadn't seen Becky in weeks. Along with Sadie, Becky had told me in trance that Sarah did not do it—and Becky was a real witch who knew things. Jerry had spent time and police station resources trying to track them with no luck whatsoever. Even the FBI was at a loss. This latest discovery seemed to prove that Harry had planned the entire thing from day one—even down to writing that note and placing it in the skeleton's hand. Other than thinking the school was still a recruitment center he had no motive. And without the interference of the ghost of Grant or Timothy many more would have been killed. I turned to Jerry and gave him a quick kiss on the mouth. "See you at home and maybe tonight you can tell me about your four months of hell."

"Maybe," Jerry said, his dark eyes meeting mine. I saw a smile behind his reluctance, the opening I'd been waiting for.

When I heard the contractor call my name I hurried back inside. He wanted to give me the good news that Tarot and Tea would be ready for business by the end of the week.

A note from the author

Keep a lookout for next Summer McCloud paranormal mystery as well as the first book of Nikki's witch series! And in the meantime here is a list of Nikki's other books:

Murder in Plain Sight
Saffron and Seaweed

The Moonstone
The Wolf Moon
Bridge of Mist and Fog

Gypsy's Quest
Gypsy's Return
Gypsy's Secret

Just Another Desert Sunset
Coyote Sunrise